PRAISE FOR

ESCAPE FROM ALGIERS

"Ted Kissel has fashioned a novel about love and longing which upends convention and defies expectations. It is a story of two lovers separated, of their desperation to reunite, and the way Kissel tells his story—fusing elements of action, spy craft, history, and the supernatural—is masterful and surprising. One senses an abiding hope and faith in the book, the sense that the power of love is both wonderfully unknowable and at the same time limitlessly rewarding for those who dare take the plunge. I suggest you take the plunge with *Escape From Algiers*."

—Alfredo Botello, Author of *180 Days*

"Ted Kissel's detailed local knowledge and deep expertise in North Africa punctuates *Escape from Algiers* and will keep readers enthralled in the adventures of Mitch Ross! If you liked *Betrayal in the Casbah*, you must get the sequel!"

—Brian J. Morra, Author of *The Able Archers* and *The Righteous Arrows*

"*Escape from Algiers* is a riveting tale of love, betrayal, and survival against the backdrop of terrorism and political intrigue. Ted's firsthand experience as a defense attaché adds a gripping authenticity, while the emotional journey of Mitch and Abella keeps readers on the edge of their seats, longing for their reunion amidst the chaos of war."

—Susan M. Burge, Commander, USN (Ret.)

"*Escape from Algiers* is a thrilling and authentic portrayal of heroism, sacrifice, and resilience in the face of relentless danger. With its pulse-pounding action, vivid depiction of counterterrorism, and an intimate understanding of military life, this gripping sequel will keep readers on the edge of their seats, eagerly rooting for Mitch and Abella as they navigate treacherous paths to find each other once again."

—Brian Anderson, Lieutenant Colonel, USAF

Escape from Algiers

by Ted Kissel

© Copyright 2024 Ted Kissel

ISBN 979-8-88824-310-7

All rights reserved. No part of this publication may be reproduced, stored in a retrieval system, or transmitted in any form or by any means—electronic, mechanical, photocopy, recording, or any other—except for brief quotations in printed reviews, without the prior written permission of the author.

This is a work of fiction. The characters are both actual and fictitious. With the exception of verified historical events and persons, all incidents, descriptions, dialogue and opinions expressed are the products of the author's imagination and are not to be construed as real.

Published by

◀ köehlerbooks™

3705 Shore Drive
Virginia Beach, VA 23455
800-435-4811
www.koehlerbooks.com

ESCAPE FROM ALGIERS

TED KISSEL

VIRGINIA BEACH
CAPE CHARLES

Frankie

To the most wonderful and loving dog.
You shall forever reside in our hearts until we meet again.

1

The ice and snow began to build along the aged walls of the gray stone and wooden buildings that ran perpendicular to the Potomac River. The sun had long since set, replaced by bone-chilling winds howling through the cobblestone streets and alleyways of the old colonial town of Alexandria, Virginia.

In the distance, three men huddled in the darkness adjacent to an Irish pub, cupping their hands around the embers of their cigarettes. Their words and periodic laughter were muffled by the wind. It didn't matter how many layers the men wore; the wind seemed to cut like a knife through every seam and buttonhole of their heavy coats. Other than the laughter and a few window shutters slamming against their frames, only the sound of the wind persisted.

Mitch had enough of the cold confinement of his wooden dwelling. It had originally been a small horse stable during America's formative years. But with time, it had been crudely converted to an austere single-room flat. The only heating was from a small wood-burning fireplace that barely warmed the room. Other than the adjacent bathroom, the fireside room was the only location in the entire flat. It embodied Mitch's living room, office, bedroom, and kitchen depending on what time of the day or night. The bathroom had only a shower, toilet, and a cracked mirror that hung awkwardly from the wall. There was no sink, and the shower curtain was torn and wrinkled. But Mitch didn't care as none of this would soon matter.

The cards were stacked against him regardless of the evidence. Whatever the outcome, he couldn't overcome the emptiness tearing at his inner being. His heart ached for those that he loved, those who had died protecting him from the terrorists. But most of all, he could barely breathe when thinking of the loss of Abella. He had loved her as he had loved no other.

From time to time, Mitch's thoughts drifted back to that last evening, as they ran from the terrorists in the Casbah. His mind would not allow him to forget as she desperately reached out to him and then she was gone. Mitch realized that he would never see her again. As far as he was concerned, the loss of Abella and his impending imprisonment would destroy any reason for living.

As he attempted to leave his flat, Mitch kicked aside the old sweatshirt that he had wedged between the door and the uneven wooden floor, a failed attempt to stop the cold draft.

What a shithole! Mitch thought as he looked around the room while pulling his heavy wool coat from a broken wooden peg that had been jammed into a crack in the wall.

I guess I should feel lucky to have found this dump in the DC area, considering I didn't have to sign a lease. Shit, I'll be fortunate if I spend two months in this ancient flophouse. At least I can get out and walk the streets at night and not be confined to a room on Bolling Air Force Base. Staying on the air base would mean constant surveillance by the security police. But regardless, they're still treating me like a damn felon, taking my passport and driver's license. I'm not stupid enough to run. I did what I had to do under the conditions that the White House and State Department had levied on me. To hell with it, that's water under the bridge now. As they say, it is what it is, and I can't go back in time. Oh God, if only I could turn back the clock.

Mitch pulled a knitted scarf from the inner sleeve of the coat and wrapped it around his neck. He had misplaced his gloves, so he shoved his hands into his coat pockets.

It had taken months to recover from the wounds he received in the Casbah. There was a small reddish scar that extended from his thick blond hair to just above the center of his forehead. The color and length of the scar seemed like a crimson pointer that made people focus on his vivid blue eyes, chiseled jawline, and weathered good looks. His right arm was still painful as he raised it to put on his coat. The bullet had passed through his shoulder, but it was the subsequent infection that had prolonged his hospital stay at Andrews Air Force Base Medical Center.

Mitch pulled the door open, and the cold wind slammed his face like a slap from an enraged lover. He lowered his shoulder into the wind as he pulled the door shut. *No need to lock it. If a thief gets in, he can take whatever he wants. There's nothing in there of value.*

As he walked into the street he cursed while slipping on the ice and snow. He grabbed an old frozen rod iron fence to steady himself, tearing away the top layer of flesh from his hand as he pulled it away. It had been years since he had felt such cold, but he needed to get out to help clear his mind. His every thought took him back to Algeria and those final moments on the narrow steps of the Casbah that ended all his dreams.

2

It had been bittersweet during those months of recovery in the medical center on the air base in Maryland. Mitch had been watched by security police twenty-four seven but had been treated well by the medical staff. His time there only delayed the inevitable doom of facing a special congressional committee investigating the failed rescue attempt of the American prisoner of war Captain Seth Hunt, who remained captive in Algeria. Mitch was responsible for the deaths of American embassy staff members who had assisted him on the botched rescue. He was certain that President Bush had been briefed of his failure and requested the investigation.

As each step into the freezing wind became more difficult, Mitch realized that his clothing was not suited for the extreme cold. From time to time he trudged through the snowpack streets and smelled cigarette smoke that traveled with the glacial wind. He glanced up and saw three men standing outside an old pub. Mitch quickly crossed the icy cobblestones and nodded to acknowledge the men without saying a word. He struggled to open the heavy wooden door of the pub as the wind resisted his efforts. With the help of one of the men outside, he finally succeeded.

The welcoming warmth of a huge stone fireplace melted the frost and ice that had formed in his eyebrows and nostrils. His shaking fingers attempted to unbutton his long woolen coat and loosen his scarf. Mitch felt relaxed while sitting at the massive bar that extended the entire length of the interior of the pub.

There were small round wooden tables with chairs placed between a tiny stage and the bar. A few diners were eating corn beef and cabbage as they drained their large mugs of beer. An Irish minstrel was tuning his guitar as he sat on a stool preparing to play. Mitch smelled the beef and remembered the exquisite dinners Djamila had prepared for Abella and him at the US Embassy in Algiers. Those magical moments that they shared were now gone. As he was lost in thought a voice pierced the deep caverns of Mitch's mind and he quickly returned to reality.

"No offense mate, but yah look like ten miles of bad road," the barkeep said with a thick Irish accent. "Lad, grab a stool here at the end of the bar. There be less steps to take and closer to your glass of liquid dinner. I be Sean Doran, straight from the emerald isles, and yah my new friend might be?"

Mitch looked up at the bartender and with a dry response. "Ross, Mitch Ross." Then he slowly stepped to the corner stool, sat, and stared at the counter without raising his head.

"Mitch, let me take yah coat. Oh, by the way, I should be thrashed for not welcoming yah to Murph's. It be the grandest pub this side of Ireland. By the looks of it, I believe yah need a good stiff one and a shoulder to lean on. What'll yah have?"

"Bourbon please, straight up."

"May there be any particular brand for yah?"

"No, just the closest you can reach. It doesn't matter. Nothing matters anymore," Mitch said while still looking down at a small crack that ran along the diameter of the bar.

The bartender grabbed the nearest bottle of bourbon and poured a generous shot into a glass. He slid a coaster under the drink and placed it in front of Mitch.

"Cheers Mitch, and please let me take that cover of yours. It be quite heavy and wet."

Mitch slid off the stool and struggled while removing his coat from his right shoulder.

He grunted as he slowly slipped it off his back.

"Lad, be easy with yah movements. Yah seem to be a man that has experienced a lot and I be the best listener in all of Alexandria, Virginia. I be more than happy to hear of yah adventures, my new friend."

Mitch lifted his coat over the bar and Sean quickly took the heavy wet item. The Irishman walked to the far side of the pub where a coat rack was near the large fireplace. He turned after hanging the coat and stepped to the small stage and whispered to the minstrel.

"Play me a soft sweet song from home. I feel that I be talkin' to a man at the bar that is as lonesome for what he misses as I be for Ireland."

"That be my pleasure, Sean," the minstrel said.

The minstrel began playing as Sean slowly walked behind the bar and toward the far end where Mitch was sitting.

"O Danny boy, the pipes the pipes are callin'. From glen to glen and down the mountainside . . ."

Mitch could feel the burn of the bourbon in his throat. But he knew that it was a good burn and one that would warm his inner being both physically and mentally.

As Sean returned and began to dry newly washed glasses, he slowly talked to Mitch as the minstrel softly sang in the background and the warm fire and booze began to work their relaxing magic.

"So, tell me Mitch, are yah crazy enough to be here on holiday or business during this Artic cold spell?"

Mitch had warmed up enough to respond with more than a few words. "I just moved into a small place around the block a few weeks ago. I was going nuts sitting in my flat tonight and had to get out. Happened to notice the guys outside smoking and thought it was time to warm up. So that's why I came in."

"Are yah originally from this area or have yah traveled a distance to arrive on the doorstep of DC?"

Normally Mitch wouldn't open up to a stranger until he knew they were trustworthy. But considering he was in the States and his give-a-shit level was extremely low, he responded openly and truthfully. "Less than a year ago I was living in North Africa working out of the US Embassy in Algiers." Mitch reached for his drink and drained the last bit of bourbon.

Sean's head jerked up while drying a glass. "I've heard that Algeria be an extremely dangerous location for anyone, but a deathtrap for a non-Muslim! Might yah be a diplomat with the State Department? Those scars and swellings about yah face, now tell me lad, they came from that dastardly country?" Before Mitch could respond, Sean poured a glass of his top-shelf bourbon.

"This be on me, Mitch. If yah served in that country and received those wounds while doing your duty, then this be the least I can do for yah."

Mitch raised the glass toward Sean. "A great American author once said, kindness is the language which the deaf can hear and the blind can see. Thanks Sean, that's very kind of you." Mitch took a long draw from the glass. "To answer your question, yes, these wounds are from Algeria. As bad as they may appear, the scars within are much worse."

Sean realized that he had gone far enough discussing Mitch's recent past. He didn't want to step over the line, so he changed the subject. "So, yah said something about liven just a few blocks away from the pub. Where might that be?"

"It's actually just a real small place across from the old Christ Church on North Washington Street."

"Hmmm, during me breaks in the warmer time of year I usually wander in that direction. I light up me smoke and watch the tourists strolling along the lanes of this wee little village. You know George use to attend church in that house of worship near where yah live. Aye, it's very old and still has the pew marked where he sat each

Sunday. Tell me Mitch, it not be that old stable flat that yah live in on Ross Alley?

Mitch was amazed that Sean knew exactly where he lived, but the statement about George threw him. *Why would Sean assume that I know who George is?* Mitch thought. "Yes, unfortunately it is that old one room former horse stable that I call home. But Sean, who's George?"

"Now lad, yah must a been sleepin' durin' the history lessons. George be President Washington. He and Martha attended in that very same church that's just a stone's throw from yah residence. Also, if yah don't mind me sayin', there be another famous family that worshipped there. Their name be Lee. Aye, the general attended Christ Church throughout his life until the war began. That be General Robert E. Lee."

Mitch had always been somewhat of a history buff, but never did it occur to him that the church near his flat was so famous. He had also noticed the old cemetery just outside the entrance of the church. A few of the gravestones were of American military soldiers from the Revolutionary War.

"Have yah been through the garden just outside the church? There be attached an interestn' cemetery. Of all the old headstones there be one army officer with the name Major Richard Phillips. Yah know, Mitch, you and he have somethin' in common. Yah both stay in that old stable flat near the church! Now I don't want tah disturb yah, and maybe yah didn't hear me, but I said yah both stay in that old stable. I hear tell that on some cold nights near the church, there are those that swear they hear the good major still yelling commands durin' battle against the British!"

Mitch was impressed that this Irishman knew so much about the history of Alexandria. *But why did Sean mention Major Phillips and the unnerving statement that we both stay in the old stable? Didn't he mean stayed?* Mitch stared at his glass filled with dark golden Kentucky magic and thought that at least for the moment thoughts of Algeria had not plagued him. Mitch was more than happy to hear about Phillips.

"I won't bore yah with details lad, but I hear tell that the good major had been in many a battle during your Revolutionary War against them British. He be an officer in the 1st Virginia Regiment. The story be told that late in the war General Washington ordered Charleston, South Carolina be defended. Major Phillips, along with the 1st Virginia, went to Charleston. Unfortunately for the Americans, the British army arrived and surrounded the city. After a wee bit of time and many casualties, the American commander in Charleston decided to surrender his army and the city to the Brits. Phillips refused his commander's order. They say that on the tenth of May 1780, the good major took his horse in the wee hours of the mornin' and rode full out through the British line. He be chased by a handful of them Brits. Regrettably, Major Phillips was hit by the ball from a British cavalryman's flintlock. Although the wound would have stopped most men, he continued ridin' until his horse was near dead. The first night he hid on a farm near Charlotte, North Carolina. The next mornin' he was given a fresh horse by the farmer and Phillips continued his journey, never stoppin' in spite of his wound. Very late that night he arrived here in Alexandria. By then the poor man be near death. I've been told Major Phillips rode to Christ Church and collapsed, falling from his horse. The good reverend of the church helped the major into the sanctuary. Then the reverend contacted the owner of a nearby stable, and arranged for the major and his horse to spend the night in the very stable that yah now reside in. The next mornin' the reverend went to the stable with food and blankets and found Major Phillips in the hayloft, dead. His war wound had finally taken his life, but he had left a note. The story be told that the note mentioned the love he had for his wife and children. Also, he wrote about praying to the Almighty that America would prevail in her struggle against the British Crown. But the most facinatin' of all that was written in the note was of a wee chest that he had hidden in the stable. The contents of the chest is unknown. Over two hundred years have passed, no one has found it or admitted to finding it. Mitch, yah know better than I, but I'm sure the hayloft no longer exists, and the old wooden walls have thinned and would not be able to hide even a mouse.

"Sean, that's quite a story. It's interesting that the owner of the flat didn't tell me anything about the history of the old stable except that it had been built prior to the Revolutionary War. Do you believe the ghost stories about Major Phillips and his chest?"

"Aye lad. The Irish tend to be quite superstitious, so me thoughts are that the good major still lurks around these parts. A few of the pub's regular patrons have said that they have heard Phillips late in the evenin' as they walked near Christ Church. But he not be an evil ghost, no not him. They say that when the moon be high in the sky and the wind is just so, they hear his orders to his men and have seen the dashing officer with his sword drawn from its scabbard. Yah landlord more than likely didn't tell yah the stories of Major Phillips because the flat had been empty for almost twelve months. I don't want yah to get a frightful feelin', but the last resident left the flat one evening without tellin' a soul. A note was found saying somethin' about the damn stable was cold, dirty, and a ghost frequently appeared!"

The effects of Mitch's bourbon immediately disappeared as he sat erect on his bar stool. "You're not bullshitting me are you, Sean? Have you personally seen or heard the ghost?"

"There be times late in the evenin' after me work shift be done, I walk to the corner near where yah live. Honestly, I have heard the man speak as clearly as we are talkin' now. I would never make up a tale of this. But you seem to be a man of intellect that will ponder what yah have heard this evenin'. I not be lying when I say, may yah know nothin' but happiness for the rest of yah life! But yah needed to know about Major Richard Phillips."

Mitch sat in silence sipping what remained of his bourbon, wondering if it was fate that had led him to the pub.

3

The 747 touched down at Dulles International and taxied to its gate. The passengers deplaned and proceeded to customs for clearance into the United States. The flight had originated in Marrakech, Morocco stopping briefly at Charles de Gaulle International and then on to the Washington DC area.

As the baggage carousel came to life, a young North African man dressed in denims and a dark green sweatshirt grabbed his small leather bag. He quickly glanced to his left noticing a middle-aged man with a grayish beard standing on the other side of the carousel. Their eye contact was fleeting, but enough to acknowledge their next task of getting through customs and meeting in Alexandria. The young man proceeded to the US customs area pulling his Moroccan passport from the back pocket of his jeans, which he handed to the customs agent. The man knew there would be questions for which he had carefully prepared.

"Are you here for business or pleasure?" the customs agent asked.

"Business. I work for a company called the Maghreb Merchants of North Africa. We import and sell handmade pottery and painted tiles from Morocco. My uncle runs the business locally in Alexandria."

The agent appeared skeptical and had been looking for short concise answers, not explanations. "How long do you plan to stay, and will it be primarily in the DC area?"

"Approximately two weeks, and it will only be in the DC Beltway area."

This guy obviously has entered the country on numerous business trips because he knows the local lingo using the term beltway. He also seems to be rather relaxed, the agent thought. But unknown to the customs agent, the young man's heart was ready to explode. *Stay calm, breath normally, and don't sweat,* the man repeated to himself while attempting to concentrate on the questions.

The agent glanced at his computer and noted that the man had been to the United States at least six times in the past year. "Okay Mr. Sadi welcome to the USA."

The young man nodded. Taking his passport, he quickly proceeded to the exit doors as the sweat began to bead on his brow and his heart continued to race. Once outside he took a deep breath, but immediately felt the frigid cold of the early December 2000 evening. He quickly hailed a cab as the freezing air retained the fog-like exhaust of the cars and buses waiting to pick up their riders. A taxi pulled up to the curb and the shivering North African quickly entered the backseat. As he sat waiting to depart, he glanced at an adjacent bus stop and noticed the long line of passengers that were stepping onto the local DC transit. As his cab slowly moved, weaving between the thick airport traffic, he noticed the man he had made eye contact while at the baggage carousel boarding a bus.

"Where you headed?" The cabbie asked as he concentrated on the traffic.

With a slight French accent the North African responded, Alexandria, 325 Cameron Street. "It is a little pottery shop called Maghreb Merchants of North Africa adjacent to Gadsby's Tavern."

The cabby nodded. "A little north off King Street. Depending on the traffic we'll be there in just under an hour."

The North African eased back into the cushioned seat of the taxi and closed his eyes. It had been a long trip and fatigue was slowly overcoming his thoughts like waves on the shore gently covering sand.

4

The middle-aged man slowly climbed the steps of the bus and handed the driver a ticket that would take him to Alexandria.

"That'll be the sixth stop prior to crossing the bridge into DC," the bus driver said as he shoved the ticket into a small tin container adjacent to the bus fare box.

The man noticed the only remaining seats were near the back of the bus. Because of the size of his large suitcase, it would have to stay in a rack just behind the driver. The man struggled lifting the case and made numerous attempts to put it onto the shelf. After his third failed attempt the bulky driver, slightly irritated, released his seatbelt, and grabbed the case flipping it onto the second level of the rack.

"Okay Mack, you can thank me later. Take a seat so we can get this bus on the road," the driver said as he returned to his seat, pulling a handle with his thick right hand that closed the bus door.

The man squeezed his way down the aisle between heavily clothed riders with their handheld baggage sticking out into his path. He pointed to a window seat, and a tired disgruntled woman stared up at him and grudgingly moved. He knew it would be a long trip and cursed himself for not taking a piss prior to boarding the bus.

I should have taken a taxi, but that wasn't part of the plan, Maashallah, he thought while contemplating that all things occur because of the wishes of Allah. Then the North African uncomfortably settled into his tiny space knowing that it would be at least two hours before reaching his destination.

- • -•

The taxi slowed and then stopped in front of the small shop on 325 Cameron Street in Alexandria. "Hey buddy, buddy! Wake up. We're at your location in old town. I never noticed this small shop before. Is it new?" the cabbie asked as he shut off the taxi meter and looked in his rearview mirror at the North African waking up from his jet-lagged slumber.

"What? Have we arrived? It seems as though I was just at the airport. Okay how much do I owe you?"

"That'll be fifty-four bucks."

The man reached into his upper coat pocket and withdrew his wallet. "Here's sixty dollars . . . and keep the change."

"Thanks buddy, and don't forget your bag," the cabbie said as the man slid out of the backseat into the frigid air.

The young man ran from the cab and quickly entered the small shop. Instantly, he felt the inviting warmth of the furnace, heard the entry bell as the shop door opened, and smelled the welcoming aroma of mint tea brewing in a back storage room. His elderly uncle heard the bell and slowly placed the small calculator he was using near a notepad full of written numbers. The old man squinted to focus on who it might be so late in the evening. His shaking thin hands reached for the spectacles that he had brought from the old country.

"Assalam alaikum!" the young man smiled, wishing his uncle peace as he opened his arms to hug the old man.

Still fumbling with his eyeglasses, the uncle recoiled from the blurry image approaching him.

"Kalfa haalik." The young man asked how his uncle was doing while taking the startled old man into his arms.

"Abassi! Abassi Sadi . . . is that you?" The old man slowly wrapped his frail arms around his nephew.

"*Naam, naam!*" Abassi replied affirmatively in Arabic while holding his uncle, knowing that this person was the last living relative he had in the world.

The old man softly pushed Abassi to arm's length, squinted, then smiled broadly, resting his head on his nephew's large strong chest. "Abassi, the world is changing, and we must abide by the wishes of Allah. Please speak English or French while in America. Many Americans begrudge anyone speaking Arabic. Right or wrong, it is what it is."

"I understand my uncle, so tell me how you are?" Abassi said in English.

"I am fine, and you look stout as an oak tree!"

"*Al hamdu lillah,*" Abassi replied, praising Allah for his good health, then realizing that he had violated the wishes of his uncle. "Forgive me uncle, but the old ways are hard to break. I promise I will not speak Arabic outside of the mosque while here in America."

"Thank you Abassi, but I only say that for your wellbeing. Again I must emphasize, there is a lot of anger toward Arabic speaking people here in the United States since Desert Storm."

"I understand my uncle and will abide by your wishes. Now, although I have only this small leather bag it contains a gift for you from Algeria."

The old man had left his homeland during the mounting terrorist unrest in the seventies. Almost three decades had passed, and although he longed to see the land he so loved, he had never returned. His only connection to Algeria was a few elderly members of his local mosque, Abassi's business trips to Alexandria, and an occasional letter. All of his family had passed away either from old age or death by terrorism, except for Abassi. Seeing his nephew was the old man's greatest gift, so he could not imagine what was hidden in the bag.

Abassi put his bag on the shop's counter and grabbed the large brass zipper near the handles. He slowly pulled the leather strap attached to the zipper and opened the bag. Among a few clothes was a small rectangular package wrapped in green paper about the size of a small book. Abassi proudly handed the gift to his uncle.

The old man slowly pulled on the paper making sure he did not tear the colored wrapping. As the paper cover released its contents the elderly man looked up at Abassi. With tears welling and the corner of his mouth trembling, he felt a flood of emotions. He looked down at the book and slowly opened the cover as the tears began to streak down his face and fall upon the countertop.

"Only you and Allah understand the treasure you have brought me," the old man said as he raised the book above his head and then to his lips, kissing it. He again opened the cover and gazed upon the name that was barely legible. Hassan Sadi had signed his name in the book over four hundred years ago. The old man's thoughts went back to when he was a very young boy seeing his father reading from this book, the Koran. But this Koran was different than any he had ever seen or used. This special treasure had been passed down through the eldest male members of the Sadi family. After Abassi's father's passing, it was he who was next in line to receive the treasured Koran. The old man once again raised the Koran to his lips and kissed the name of the original Sadi of the family. He turned to Abassi. "Never could I have envisioned such a special moment as this. Let us celebrate with the blessings of Allah, and a small measuring of French brandy that I have not touched since leaving my beloved *ville blanche*, Algiers."

The old man bent and opened a small cabinet door near his right knee. Reaching down he took a dusty ancient bottle of brandy and two small glasses. Abassi could tell by the dust and yellow label that it had rested in the cabinet for decades. The old man held the glasses and blew out the dust. He knew it would be difficult to remove the old cork and handed it to Abassi. The young man carefully looked at the dry rotted cork and began to slowly turn the fragile plug. It disintegrated as he turned and most of the small fragments fell into the bottle.

"I am sorry uncle." Abassi said, looking at the bottle and then back to his uncle.

"It is not a problem," the old man replied. With his shaking hand he carefully poured the brandy through a small piece of cloth to catch the particles of cork as the golden liquid entered the glass. He poured another and handed it to Abassi.

"May Allah bless the remaining two members of the family of Sadi. Salute!"

With that said, they raised and touched their glasses. Then putting the brandy to their lips they made one quick flick of the wrist, and it was gone.

"Uncle, will I be staying in the same room on the second floor?"

"Yes Abassi, and when Farid Benzai arrives, he will be in the adjoining room to yours."

"Excellent, but Farid took the bus and won't arrive for at least another hour," Abassi informed his uncle. He grabbed his bag, entered the storage room, and climbed the steps to the second floor.

5

Two gray seagulls gracefully glided just above the white caps. They followed each other, skimming low over the water's surface and following the contours of the waves and then soared skyward as they approached the rocky cliffs. The silver dome of the Basilica reflected the sunlight as the early morning breeze softly blew from the Mediterranean Sea. The strikingly beautiful Notre Dame d' Afrique in Algeria stood on the cliff as a lonesome beacon of Christianity in a land of Islam. The two seagulls rose high above the Basilica and then perched on the cross atop the dome.

Mother Superior stood beneath a tree gazing out over the Mediterranean, praying the rosary, and watching the seagulls climb and circle above the house of worship. Once she had finally praised and thanked God, Mother Superior turned toward the Basilica and rapidly walked to the large wooden doors that led to the beautiful sanctuary within.

"Pere.... Pere puis-je avoir un moment?" The senior nun requested to speak to the archbishop.

"Why of course Mother Superior, but let us speak in English because of the arrival of the new nuns from South Africa. We need the practice. Now, is there something troubling you?"

"Perhaps Father, but can we talk in private?"

"Yes, let's go to my office." The archbishop genuflected to the

Blessed Sacrament as Mother Superior mirrored his actions and then rose and walked to a small door adjacent to the alter. Entering the dark stale room the archbishop motioned for Mother Superior to sit in an old wooden chair as he sat behind a worn battered bureau. Other than those pieces and a crucifix on the wall behind the archbishop, the room was empty except for a couple of books, papers, and a small lamp on the desktop.

"Now tell me what troubles you," the archbishop softly said while folding his hands on the old desk.

"Father, it has to do with one of our novices training to become a nun. First, let me say that she is far superior in intellect and personality than all the other novices. When she is directed to accomplish a task, there is no doubt that it will be completed magnificently."

"If this is your definition of a problem or issue then we must change jobs, Mother Superior! But putting all joking aside, what is the problem? The novice seems to be an outstanding future nun. Is she reluctant to take her temporary vows?"

"No Father, it is none of that. It's that she has an edge about her that surfaces on occasion and I can't completely identify why. Other than that she is everything that I would ever hope that a nun would be. God has blessed her with so many gifts. She is naturally beautiful, energetic, charismatic, multilingual, and very athletic. But I feel that something is wrong. When I look deep into her eyes I see a great sadness. It is as if she has experienced a great deal of pain and has lost so much in her life. At times she has little patience with the other novices. Especially when they discuss the difficulties of life. She never hesitates to tell them how sheltered their lives are. Father, there is a great sorrow that resides in her heart, and I continuously pray for her."

"Mother Superior, it is good that you pray for her. I have noticed that the novice you are referring to never leaves the Basilica when there is an outing for all of you. She stays within the walls of Notre Dame d' Afrique praying and crying while all of you are gone. It is as if she is afraid to journey outside of the protective walls of the

Basilica. Please have her come see me."

"Thank you Father. I will have her report to your office immediately. I worry for her wellbeing." Mother Superior bowed to the archbishop and departed.

Instead of reentering the sanctuary, she stepped down to a dark, narrow, dingy corridor that led to that portion of the Basilica that had been converted to a convent. At that time of the morning the novices and nuns were having fellowship. As Mother Superior entered a large room that resembled a military barracks, they all stood. She quickly scanned the room until she noticed the one troubled novice standing near her bunk dressed impeccably in her habit.

Mother Superior pointed at her and said, "Please come with me."

"As you wish, Mother Superior." The novice joined Mother Superior as they departed the convent.

"Mother Superior, is there something wrong that I should be concerned about."

"No, my little lamb, don't be concerned. The archbishop would like a short chat as he does with all the nuns and novices from time to time."

They approached the archbishop's office and gently knocked on the door.

"Please enter."

The novice bowed to the archbishop as Mother Superior closed the door and departed to rejoin the others in the convent.

"Please sit. I have been told great things about you and your progress to become a nun."

"Thank you, Father. That is gratifying to hear such kind words."

"I requested that you come to my office so we can discuss an issue that is long overdue."

The novice felt a sickening nervousness in her stomach that made her swallow hard and squirm in her chair. The archbishop walked to the door to make certain it was tightly shut. He returned to his seat behind the large wooden bureau and stared at her as he folded his hands and leaned forward.

"What I am about to say may never leave this room. Do you understand?"

The novice immediately sat up, wide-eyed. "Yes Father, I will say nothing of what we are to discuss."

"Thank you. Undoubtedly you have seen the crypts of your French ancestors that are buried within the walls and floor of this magnificent Basilica. They were of the original French colonists who came to Algeria in the 1830s. It is an honor for me to know that you are of that bloodline.

"I remember you as a very young girl while attending mass here at the Basilica with your mother. Although it was—and is—extremely dangerous to attend mass, because of the terrorist activity in this area, you have always been a part of this Catholic establishment.

"Now let me be very honest with you. I know quite well that you are not here to become a nun! I am well aware of what you and the American Defense Attaché Colonel Ross attempted to do in the Casbah a number of months ago. Unfortunately, you were involved in a very dangerous activity that resulted in the deaths of many. What you were attempting to accomplish did not succeed. The team that you were a member failed to rescue Captain Seth Hunt, the American prisoner of war.

"I know this because of what I have read, what I have heard, but most of all from my discussions with an acquaintance of yours. Colonel Yves Dureau, the French defense attaché, and I have met on numerous occasions during diplomatic receptions and dinners. We have agreed, for your safety, that you will remain here. He and I, with the help of the Vatican and French government, are working to obtain a visa for you. Hopefully, a visa to France, but it is my understanding that more important to you is a visa to America. Colonel Dureau mentioned to me that you and the American Colonel are very close. But unfortunately, he is presently in the United States. I cannot guarantee that we will succeed in acquiring visas for you.

"I have learned there are falsehoods that have been inserted in your records by al-Qaeda's Algerian GSPC terrorist group and corrupt government officials. But please understand that you will always be protected here at the Basilica. No one else but you, I, and Colonel Dureau know why you are here. All the others in this house of worship assume that you are a novice in training to become a nun. I must say Abella, you are doing exceedingly well. The only negative comment made by Mother Superior concerns your edginess. But that is understandable considering what you have gone through in your life and during the failed rescue operation in the Casbah.

"Father, if I may comment. I had no clue who within the walls of this Basilica knew my story. Colonel Dureau said nothing to me other than I would be living and training inside the safety of this sanctuary. Thank you so much for your understanding and assistance. The church has always been my refuge in times of crisis, and now it is the only safe location I have left in Algeria. If I leave the confines of these walls, I will be murdered by the GSPC. They know that I was part of the embassy team that killed many of their members in the Casbah. I'm scared Father. I cry a lot, but only when the others are not around. Also, there is a deep void that remains in my heart. I love Colonel Ross and long to be with him."

Tears flowed as she paused with her head bowed to regain her composure. Her fingers probed a small hidden pocket in her habit for a ring that Mitch had given her during their final moments together.

There was silence as the archbishop was deep in thought and Abella continued to quietly weep. He reflected on the misfortunes that she had experienced after returning to Algeria from the United States. He remembered reading of the assassination of her father and the subsequent death of her mother a year later. The archbishop was also aware that Abella had graduated from Georgetown University's school of nursing in Washington DC, while her father was the Algerian deputy defense attaché in America. He also recalled that Colonel Dureau had mentioned that Abella was a very competent nurse and marksman, especially under the most dreadful conditions while battling terrorists.

"There is no doubt that you have tragically lost a great deal in your young life. Believe me when I say that you are in my thoughts and prayers daily. I truly hope that one day I will be able to tell you that God has fulfilled your dreams and that you can leave Algeria for America. But until that time, God wants you here in training to become a nun."

Abella was astonished. Never had she seriously contemplated that she would have to remain at the Basilica and complete the training to become a num. That would take years, and she knew that she could not commit to the final vows marrying her to God and the church. She felt a burn in her stomach as she tried to control her tears and trembling.

"I am sorry if I have upset you Abella with my words. But I must be completely honest.

Only God knows what is to be. Pray to the Almighty that he will bless and protect you."

Abella knew that she had spent more than enough of the archbishop's time. Also, the other novices and nuns would begin to wonder why the counseling session was taking so long. As Abella bowed to the archbishop and left his office she thought, *I've got to come up with a believable excuse why I was with the archbishop for almost an hour. They will think that I'm having second thoughts of being here. Actually, that wouldn't be too far from the truth.*

6

The chairman struck the gavel on the highly polished table. "Will the committee please come to order." Approximately twenty-eight congressional members of both the House and Senate sat behind and on either side of Senator Carl Levin of New Jersey. The chamber was cavernous, located across from the House Chamber. The row of seating behind Chairman Levin was elevated, similar to a sports stadium, giving those senators and representatives an unobstructed view of Colonel Mitch Ross.

Mitch stood adjacent to a small, isolated desk, feeling very alone, while facing the committee. A large silver microphone was placed directly in front of him, as was a pitcher of water, one glass, and a notebook.

My God, now I know how lonely and scared the Christians felt in the coliseum when the Romans released the lions! Mitch thought as he gazed upon the committee.

Once the members of the committee took their seats and settled in for the opening remarks by Chairman Levin, Mitch stood to be sworn in.

"Please take your seat Colonel." Senator Levin stated while scornfully glaring at Mitch.

Mitch was wearing his blue Air Force service dress uniform with his pilot wings and a chest full of ribbons above the left pocket. On the right side was a large round Defense Intelligence Agency medallion accompanied by the Office of the Secretary of Defense badge. His defense attaché silver aiguillette ropes, which identified him as a military diplomat, went around his left shoulder and cascaded across the front left side of his coat. The aiguillette terminated at the top main button of his tunic along the middle of his chest. His colonel's rank was affixed to epaulets on each of his shoulders. The collar of his light blue shirt had been firmly starched, and his tie had been fashioned into a half Windsor knot. His slacks were exceptionally pressed, and the seams appeared to be razor sharp. The intense lightning in the chamber reflected off Mitch's shoes like black mirrors. His blond hair had been cut short but still retained a wavy thickness. He resembled every aspect of a proud military officer.

"I as the chairman of this esteem special Congressional Investigation Committee want to thank you, Colonel Ross, for your service to our great country," Levin started. "It is humbling to read of your sacrifices in combat and service in far off lands protecting our American freedoms. But we are not here to discuss your service record, but to investigate what happened during the failed attempt to rescue an American prisoner of war, Captain Seth Hunt. We want to know how a highly classified operation could fail so miserably. How that failure resulted in the loss of US Embassy staff members and the wounding of others, to include yourself, Colonel. What was to be a small covert operation in the Casbah of Algiers has now become a great embarrassment to the United States. An embarrassment not only here on Capitol Hill, but also worldwide. The failure of this operation rests completely and totally on your shoulders, Colonel Ross. This story is not a pleasant one as it will unfold in these proceedings.

"The members of this committee will undoubtedly ask how this could have happened and demand that it never happen again. Personally, I must add that this mission should never have occurred at all in the manner it was planned out by you. As chairman of the Senate Intelligence Committee, it is the accepted practice and policy that we are to have advanced notification of any covert operation carried out by the United States. But despite these policies, the classified plans, and events that you, Colonel Ross, concocted were never reported to my Senate committee. Thus, your mission subsequently exploded into a dismal failure. You knowingly worked outside the system and used unconventional channels and individuals that were accountable to no one.

"This escapade that you carried out was both sad and wretched. It was filled with recklessness and unspeakable conduct. This hearing has been established in an effort to find the facts so as not to repeat the mistakes. To this end, we will deal with questions of who authorized the operations, why wasn't Congress advised of the mission, who devised this undertaking, what was the approval process, why weren't special operation forces utilized, and were you operating under a unique foreign policy that this esteem group of congressmen and women are not aware of? Once these questions are truthfully answered, then we will have a better idea of why this mission was such a disaster. So with that said, I call this hearing to order."

Mitch attempted to pour water from a pitcher into the glass, his hands noticeably shaking. *Shit! I can't do this. I'm too damn nervous. I'll spill water all over my uniform and the floor.* Mitch slowly set the pitcher down and tightly gripped the pen next to the notepad to steady his hand and calm his racing heart.

Senator Levin paused, whispered to a colleague seated on his right, and then looked across the room to the solitary desk where Mitch sat. "At this particular moment would you, Colonel Ross, wish to address the committee?"

As Mitch repositioned the microphone, he tasted the sour acid in his stomach and the dryness of his mouth. "Thank you, Mr. Chairman." Mitch stated as he swallowed hard. "As you all know, I'm Mitchell Ross, colonel, United States Air Force. After serving over two decades in the Air Force, I was assigned to the Defense Intelligence Agency and subsequently entered defense attaché training. As an attaché working out of a US Embassy, it was my job to build military relations with the host country. That consisted of bilateral training, planning, and executing war games, and military equipment sales. I was also responsible for gathering information that would be vital to our intelligence agencies and the safety and defense of our nation and its citizens. But my responsibilities extended beyond those that I have mentioned. As a member of the military, I ultimately serve the president of the United States. He is my commander in chief, and I carry out his orders explicitly. The president is well aware that America exists in a dangerous world that harbors those that desire to destroy our country. I have always maintained the mindset, as a military officer, that mission accomplishment is paramount. I didn't volunteer for the covert operation to rescue Captain Seth Hunt. I was directed to do it. But being an action-oriented individual, I relished the challenge. I acted upon that challenge because my superiors, my chain of command, had requested that I take on the risks of the mission. There were obstacles in planning the operation primarily because I was not to use special operational forces or clandestine intelligence agencies. I was told to keep the operation as low-key as possible. I and my team worked extremely hard to minimize the obstacles and problems that we anticipated would occur during the mission.

"Now looking back, I realize that in some aspects of the planning we succeeded, and in others we failed. But I will always hold my head high with pride that as a team we gave it our best shot. I will never have regrets thinking of this mission other than those that we lost. You here, members of the Congressional Investigation Committee, will decide what is considered acceptable and unacceptable. Ultimately you will make the final decision on my future, my Air Force career, and my life. These months since the operation in the Casbah have been extremely difficult for me. Not just the months spent recovering from my wounds, but the mental anguish of reliving every moment of that difficult day.

"Many of you sitting in front of me have already decided that

I'm guilty of inept leadership and poor planning. That my failure resulted in the deaths of extraordinary embassy members. Some of you undoubtedly consider me a rogue military officer that was out of control and reported to no one. I'm not ashamed of my professional and personal behavior while carrying out this operation. I tried to the best of my ability, as did every member of my team, to successfully accomplish the rescue. In closing, Mr. Chairman, I only ask that once the truth be known, that you and this esteem committee admit that perhaps your initial assumptions concerning the operation and my leadership were wrong. Thank you."

Senator Levin sneered at Mitch then slowly and sarcastically said, "Thank you for your remarks, Colonel Ross."

Just as Levin was to make another remark an intern entered the room from a back door and quickly walked directly to the senator, handing him a small note with a short-handwritten message. The intern immediately turned and disappeared through the door he had entered.

As the room fell silent, Mitch felt calm, drinking water from his glass without jitters.

A low murmur rose among members of the committee as they quietly discussed their thoughts of Mitch's remarks. Levin slowly read the note given to him by the intern and stared at the presidential seal above the written words for a lengthy period of time. He seemed to be deep in thought as a colleague leaned over and whispered to him, snapping the committee chairman out of his trance. He jotted a few notes and then pressed a button on his microphone.

"At this time, the questioning will begin. I will determine who will speak by the indication of a green light that corresponds to your seating. The column of lights is on the back wall located behind Colonel Ross." Senator Levin muffled his cough while grabbing for his glass of water. Then he continued, "I now recognize the honorable senator from the state of New York, Daniel Moynihan.

"Thank you, Mr. Chairman. Colonel Ross, being a veteran myself,

I'm aware of your sacrifices and what it means to this country. But there are times when we must reflect on our actions and determine if they were right or wrong. I have not only read, but studied, your after-action report and the comments made by the Algerian authorities. Also, I had personally talked to the former US Ambassador to Algeria before his untimely retirement from the State Department. Now, let me get to the point of my questions," Moynihan paused.

"I find it extremely interesting and perhaps somewhat reckless, the unrestrained freedoms given to you to carry out this clandestine rescue operation. Especially considering, with all due respect, all of your combat experiences occurred in the air and not on the field of battle. Therefore, I must ask who was involved, other than yourself, in the planning of this operation, why you selected them, and what was the approval process?"

Mitch cleared his voice, pressed the button on his microphone, and began his reply. "Senator, the planning for this mission began almost immediately following the US ambassador and the chief of station's briefing in the embassy. Their briefing primarily covered the background and whereabouts of Captain Seth Hunt. They described how Captain Hunt was shot down during a combat mission and his history as a POW since the end of Desert Storm in 1991. I also learned of his last known location that was somewhere in the Casbah region of Algiers."

"Excuse me, Colonel, but I'm not familiar with the title chief of station?" Senator Moynihan interrupted.

Mitch quickly responded, "That is the title given to the individual in charge of the CIA office in the embassy."

"Thank you, Colonel Ross. Please continue."

"To answer your question sir, over the weeks that followed my meeting in the embassy, I began to confirm that which had been briefed to me by the ambassador and the chief of station. Because of the covert nature of the operation and the constraints imposed on me, I had to build a team primarily from within the US Embassy.

My military administrative specialist, Chief Warrant Officer David McQueen, had spent almost twenty years as a US Army Ranger and Airborne Paratrooper. His specialty had been in tactical and strategic planning. Therefore, he was invaluable at planning, briefing, and spearheading the operation. Incidentally, Chief Warrant McQueen was an expert marksman, the best shot at the embassy. He proved his abilities with a handgun winning an embassy shooting competition against a US State Department senior special agent. Also, Chief Warrant McQueen had participated in numerous combat operations. One of which occurred in Mogadishu, Somalia in October of 1993. Senator, you most likely are familiar with that action because it became a bestselling novel entitled, *Black Hawk Down*. Dave McQueen lost half his left leg fighting for his life in the Battle of Mogadishu. But that did not encumber him as he was able to walk and run without others knowing of his handicap."

"Colonel Ross, I know that one of your wounds was a severe blow to the head during your attempted rescue mission in the Casbah. But are you aware that Chief Warrant Officer McQueen was killed in action during your failed operation?" Senator Moynihan glared into the colonel's eyes.

Mitch knew that Dave McQueen had been wounded while running from Captain Seth Hunt's house, but he was unaware that Dave had died. Mitch's last memory of McQueen was seeing him strewn on a floor losing consciousness while another team member had frantically tried to help him. Hearing of McQueen's death was too much for Mitch. He felt an intense pain in his heart and realized he was losing the battle to control his emotions. Mitch slowly lowered his head and closed his eyes, sobbing. He dabbed his eyes with a hankie. *My God please no, why did it have to be Dave. It's all my fault! I should have fought to get back to him after Abella and I joined up with Yves and Jake during the fight.* Mitch sat quietly, breathing deeply to calm himself and to show decorum. He raised his head, sat up, and squared his shoulders while responding to Senator Moynihan.

"No sir, I was not aware that Chief Warrant Officer McQueen had died of his wounds. He was a great American patriot, and I shall miss him for the rest of my life."

Senator Levin quickly interrupted. "Let's take a thirty-minute recess."

Mitch slumped in his chair rubbing his throbbing forehead attempting to tune out the voices of the congressional committee members as they moved about the room. He closed his eyes and thought about Dave McQueen, wondering what it must have been like during his last moments of life.

"Colonel Ross, do you have a minute?"

The voice was familiar and gentle. It reminded him of Abella as she would whisper during evenings together while watching sunsets over the Bay of Algiers.

Mitch immediately sat up and turned to see a young slender woman in her mid-thirties. She was dressed professionally in a dark gray business skirt and coat, along with a white blouse. Her angelic skin, reddish-golden hair, and emerald-green eyes reminded him of what he had always envisioned an attractive Irish woman to be. Mitch slowly stood as she reached out and shook his hand.

"I'm so sorry to bother you during this intense hearing. But when you became emotional after finding out that your colleague had died, it broke my heart. I don't usually talk to anyone while attending hearings. I normally have my head down frantically taking notes," she said while looking at Mitch and still holding his hand.

As Mitch attempted to release her grip he asked, "And you are a congresswoman?"

"Oh no, I'm terribly sorry. I'm Colleen Duffy of the *Washington Post*."

The Washington Post! Oh shit, she'll be picking my brain to get a story. Mitch looked at her note pad and pen firmly clenched in her left hand.

"I can't make any comments to the press at this time."

"I really didn't approach you to get a story. I just wanted you to know that I've never seen a career military man breakdown like you did during a congressional investigation. It really touched me, and I was overwhelmed with emotion and had to tell you how I felt. I'm sorry to have bothered you." She turned and walked toward the one row of seats along the wall behind Mitch's desk.

As he watched her walk away, Mitch sensed the genuine sentiment in the reporter's words. "Miss, I'm not having the greatest day at the moment. Please forgive me for being so rude."

She stopped and turned, then smiled at Mitch while nodding her acknowledgment.

Senator Levin returned to his seat and keyed his microphone. "Will the delegates of the investigation committee please return to your seats." As he waited, the chairman gazed upon the note he had placed near the microphone. He carefully unfolded the single page and ran his index finger over the embossed presidential seal, quietly staring at the words.

After all of the members of the committee had taken their seats, Levin focused on Mitch. "Let us resume the questioning. I believe Colonel Ross was explaining to the committee those that had contributed to his plan. Please proceed, Colonel."

"To continue my explanation of what went into the planning of the mission, I realized that I needed a skilled professional in close quarters urban warfare. The senior security agent at the embassy, Jake Davis, was well known as one of the best in the State Department. I was fortunate to enlist his expertise. As far as an in depth understanding of the terrorists we were facing, the French Intelligence Service had been the go-between tracking terrorist organizations in the former North African French colonies. They had infiltrated the different terrorist groups with informants who kept the French aware of Captain Seth Hunt's whereabouts. My connection to the French Intelligence Service was Colonel Yves Dureau, the French defense attaché. He kept me updated on all the latest information gathered by their intelligence service. Plus, he was willing to participate in all activities to include our rescue attempt of Captain Hunt.

"To confirm Captain Hunt's actual location within the Casbah, I unexpectedly discovered that my embassy cook had noticed, on numerous occasions, a European-looking man residing near her father's home. Although his unique garb consisted of flowing robes like that of Lawrence of Arabia, he was surrounded by casually dressed guards during his daily afternoon walk to the mosque for prayer."

"That's all fine and good Colonel, but who planned the operation?" Senator Moynihan huffed.

"Sir, each member contributed their individual piece of the plan, but Chief Warrant McQueen and I put those pieces together." Mitch's jaw tightened as he fought to suppress his growing anger at the antagonistic inquiry.

"Thank you, Colonel. Mr. Chairman, I have no further questions at this time."

Senator Levin looked beyond Mitch at the panel of lights on the wall. "The chairman recognizes the honorable representative from the State of California, Representative Brown."

"Thank you, Senator Levin. Colonel Ross, your service to American is quite commendable and I thank you for it. My questions are quite simple. Who ultimately approved of the operation, and what was the approval process?"

"Sir, I believe I mentioned earlier today and in my after-action report that the approval came from the highest level, the White House. The path of approval was the president through the secretaries of State and Defense, then finally down to the US Ambassador in Algeria."

"Yes Colonel, you had briefly mentioned something about the approval process. But I wanted to make sure that it was specifically spelled out and was recorded in the formal records of this investigation. So am I to assume that the ultimate approval of your plan came from the president?"

"Yes Sir, the final approval came from the White House. Prior to the operation, I would update the ambassador with information, and he would relay that data to the secretaries and president."

"Fine Colonel, but now I will add another question. Why wasn't Congress advised of the mission prior to its implementation? Aren't you aware of how our democracy works? Those special members of their respective congressional intelligence committees must be notified of clandestine operations prior to their execution by the military!"

"I'm well aware of the notification process sir, but notifying Congress was well above my pay grade. That responsibility should have been carried out by the respective secretaries of State and Defense. But ultimately the responsibility was with the president."

"Did you ever inquire, through your chain of command, whether Congress was being informed, Colonel?"

"No sir, I did not. As I stated, it was the authorities above me that held that responsibility."

"So you basically blew it off!"

"Sir, there is a chain of command, and at each level there are responsibilities. As I have stated, it was not at my level of responsibility to notify Congress!"

"Colonel, you are an intelligent officer. I know that you are well aware that at times you must bypass your chain of command if that chain is violating proper procedures. You should have notified those that would have contacted the appropriate congressional authorities. Mr. Chairman, I have no additional questions."

"Excuse me Representative Brown, but with all due respect, if you had read my after- action report you would have found the answer to your question. When the US ambassador was briefing me in the embassy bubble, he stated specifically that intelligence information concerning Captain Seth Hunt was being passed on to the president and the Senate Intelligence Committee. Therefore, the president and the Intelligence Committee that Senator Levin chairs, agreed that all information gathered would be kept at the highest classified level. As opposed to the apparent opinions of many members in this room, to include Senator Levin, Congress was notified, and information was passed to the Senate Intelligence Committee prior to the operation commencing. But as I stated earlier, at my level it was not my responsibility to directly notify the president or Congress!"

Mitch realized his response to the congressman had been harsh and sounding defensive. But if this committee was out to hang him then he was going to make sure that the truth was recorded. Unfortunately, at that moment there was something else that Mitch was struggling with. His pulse was rapidly rising as a searing pain quickly grew from behind his left eye. He was slowly graying out and was momentarily blinded by his extreme stress. It was the same eye that had been severely damaged by the blow from a terrorist. In his mind he was reliving his encounter with the extremists in the ancient Roman city of Tipasa, Algeria. As he sat before the congressional interrogators, he visualized his meeting with the terrorists in the ruins of the amphitheater of the gladiators, being forced to his knees, feeling the blow by the terrorist that broke his left eye socket, and finally hearing the gun shot from Abella's pistol.

Mitch's indictment of the president, secretaries, and Senate Intelligence Committee had caused the room to explode with discussions among members of Congress facing him. Others in attendance quickly scribbled notes and passed them to their aides and interns who then literally ran from the room to deliver what had just been recorded. The few members of the press, including Colleen Duffy, frantically scribbled on their notepads.

The decorum of the investigating committee had turned to complete disorder. Members were raising their voices arguing about a potential cover-up. Those few members of the press were now moving throughout the room asking pointed questions. They wanted to know what the Senate Intelligence Committee members knew or didn't know about the rescue mission. Representative Brown quickly departed the room without notifying the chairman. Senator Levin was slamming his gavel on the table attempting to gain control of the chaotic situation. All while Mitch was still imprisoned by his painful traumatic recollections.

"Are you okay, Colonel Ross?" a distant voice whispered to Mitch as he felt a hand rubbing along his upper left arm and shoulder. Slowly, his mind escaped from Tipasa, and he was back in the room of the investigation committee. He attempted to focus on the person leaning over him but could only make out a blurred shape.

"Actually, I . . . I'm not feeling well at all," Mitch responded while rubbing his eyes trying to clear his vision. Gradually the pain from behind his left eye subsided, and he again tried to focus on the individual now placing a glass of water in his right hand.

"Thank you, you're very kind."

"Please try to drink some water."

Mitch could feel the warm breath of the person near his cheek. As he slowly regained his vision Mitch realized that it was a woman with reddish-golden hair and green eyes. "Colleen, is that you?"

"Yes Colonel, in all the chaos I looked over and noticed that you had slumped in your chair and appeared to be in extreme discomfort. You had such a painful look on your face. I thought perhaps you were having a stroke. It scared me."

"What's going on? I must have lost consciousness. Why is this place out of control and Senator Levin continues to pound on the table with his gavel?"

"It was your last statement to Representative Brown that sent this room into mayhem."

"I can't remember what I said."

"Colonel, it was great! You slam dunked those arrogant congressional members."

"I want this room to come to order, now!" Senator Levin demanded as he frantically continued to strike the gavel on the table. "This is an abomination, and I will not tolerate it!"

Slowly the members of the Congressional Investigation

Committee took their seats. It was obvious that many had departed for their offices to make sure that any press releases did not implicate them in a cover-up. Once Senator Levin gained control of the hearing, he noted the absence of many members.

"Before there is a resumption of this investigation, I will warn every member that outbursts such as what I have just observed will not be tolerated! We will maintain decorum and preserve the dignity of Congress."

Mitch could still feel a slight pain near his eye, but now his thoughts kept returning to Colleen's comments. *Damn, whatever I said turned this hearing on its head. Levin will have to go into recovery mode to get back on track.* He slowly turned and noticed Colleen sitting behind and to the right of his desk against the wall.

"Because of what has just occurred, I as the chairman adjourn this investigation until tomorrow morning at nine. All members will be seated, and we will continue the questioning at that time." Senator Levin struck the gavel one more time and then carefully picked up the president's note, placing it in the upper inside pocket of his suit coat.

Mitch could feel the stress and pressure fade as he paused to allow the majority of the congressional members to depart. Finally, he stood and proceeded to the exit. Once stepping outside of the building, he felt the cold December wind and noticed how it blew along the snow- covered streets of DC. He looked down at the vast marble steps that appeared icy, and cautiously navigated each until he was in the frozen gardens of Capitol Hill. As he hesitated for a moment, Mitch attempted to recall what had happened during the hearing, his mind in a haze as he headed toward a group of oak trees in the direction of a metro train station. While passing the trees he came upon a few gray ice-covered rose bushes. Mitch thought of the warm sundrenched beautiful roses far away in the US Embassy in Algiers. Then from behind one of the tall oak trees Colleen Duffy stepped out and smiled.

"Colonel, I promise I won't ask you any questions concerning today's hearing." She patted her briefcase that contained all her notes. "I was thinking of your health and how you would negotiate the snow-covered steps of the Capitol, considering all the stress you experienced today."

"Actually, I'm feeling much better now that I'm away from all that congressional buffoonery. Oh by the way, that statement I just made is definitely off the record," Mitch said as he smiled and then laughed.

"It's good to see this side of you, Colonel. I've never really been associated with the professional military, so there is a mindset that you're a bunch of robotic types who tend to be demanding and dictatorial."

"Well, there might be some truth to what you just said, but I don't fit that category anymore. Once I climbed down from the cockpit for the last time and became a military diplomat my outlook on life changed. Also, please call me Mitch."

Colleen smiled and moved closer as she felt much more relaxed. "How is your head and the pain?"

"Better, but nothing that a good glass of bourbon can't cure."

"So, you like to drink that Kentucky magic?"

Mitch's head snapped up and his demeanor instantly became somber. Colleen realized she had obviously said something wrong.

"I . . . I'm terribly sorry. I didn't mean it in a bad way."

Mitch reached out resting his hand on her arm. "Don't worry, you didn't say anything wrong. It's just that you used a term that one of my best friends at the embassy frequently used. Jake Davis enjoyed a good glass of bourbon and a Cuban cigar from time to time. I miss him. Unfortunately, the last time I recall being with Jake, he had been severely wounded in the Casbah and I was attempting to rescue him. I don't know what happened to him. I was struck in the head by a terrorist. I don't know if Jake made it out alive. Since returning to the States I've been ordered, because of the congressional investigation, to contact no one that might have information about the failed rescue attempt. Unfortunately, I know nothing of those that were with me in Algeria."

Colleen could see the deep pain return to Mitch, and she touched his hand still resting on her arm. "Mitch, I must confess that as a reporter I tried to do as much homework as possible before sitting in the hearings. It might amaze you what a reporter discovers without violating any rules related to classified information. Also, you've not asked me for facts about the happenings in Algeria. Therefore, you've not violated the orders given to you. Your friend, Jake Davis, survived that evening in the Casbah. The report I read stated that he was rescued by security members from the US Embassy."

"WHAT! Jake is alive! Oh thank God in Heaven. Where is he?"

"I don't know where he is. The report stated that he survived the rescue attempt of Captain Hunt but sustained serious wounds. It didn't elaborate beyond that. I'm sorry."

Mitch wanted to hug Colleen but knew that wouldn't be right. He realized that he was still touching her arm and slowly removed his hand. He looked deep into her green eyes,

"There's no need for you to be sorry. What you've told me is the best news I've heard for a long, long time! Thank you so much, it really has put a positive note on what otherwise was a shitty day. Well, let me rephrase that statement. It had been a shitty day until you strolled into it."

Mitch smiled but didn't want to say anymore. He didn't want to lead her on because his love for Abella still burned deep within his heart.

"Well Colonel . . . I mean Mitch, I'm sure you need to get going and not be bothered by this crazy reporter while standing in the snow and ice."

"You're not bothering me, and by all means you're not crazy. To be honest, this is a first for me, talking to such an attractive reporter in the frozen gardens of Capitol Hill. Thanks again for being so kind during my tough moments in that hearing room."

Colleen smiled and blushed at his comment as Mitch considered inviting her to join him for a drink in one of the nearby DC watering holes. As he looked at her, he began to think of the potential political fallout if they were seen together alone at night. *Hmmmm, not a good idea Mitch Ross. You'd be sticking out like a sore thumb wearing this uniform in a DC bar just waiting to be ambushed by the gossip magazine paparazzi. They'd love to scoop a story of a colonel involved in a highly publicized congressional hearing sharing drinks with a good-looking news reporter. That wouldn't bode well for what little remains of my military career.*

"Will I see you tomorrow morning at nine for the next round of hearings?"

"Well Mitch, I believe that'll happen! But if you don't mind me asking, would you like to grab a cup of coffee at that little café across the street tomorrow morning, say at seven-thirty? It'll be my treat."

Yikes, she's too comfortable and too damn attractive, Mitch thought before blurting, "That'd be great! I'll definitely look forward to our morning rendezvous." He immediately felt uncomfortable knowing that he had stepped over the line with his enthusiastic reply.

"Great, that makes two of us!" Colleen said with a broad smile as she reached out and touched Mitch's hand before she turned and hailed a cab.

Mitch stood and watched her enter the taxi as she waved at him before the car sped down Independence Avenue and turned out of sight.

7

The name on the street sign was obscured by snow as Mitch leaned into the cold wind while heading to L'Enfant Plaza metro station. As he approached the entry escalator and descended on its stairs, he felt the warmth of the underground station. The commuter rush hour had passed, and Mitch could relax while waiting for the train. The combination of the subterranean warmth and lack of travelers jostling him made for a pleasant pause after his extremely intense day. As he was lost in thought, the station's computerized voice announced the train's arrival. He was pleasantly surprised to see a relatively empty train. He quickly entered the opened doors and found a location far from any of the other riders. He slumped into the hard plastic seat and leaned against the interior side of the train's window, pulling his coat tighter around his chilled body and closing his eyes.

As the train departed fatigue began to overtake him, and he slowly slipped into a deep sleep. He knew that it would be at least thirty minutes on the blue line before his stop at King Street station in Alexandria. His body was soothed by the syncopation of the movement of the train. Just before crossing the Potomac River and entering Arlington, it stopped at Foggy Bottom station near George Washington University. Mitch was still sleeping until a large woman with numerous shopping bags and wearing a tattered foul-smelling woolen coat flopped down hard next to him. The impact startled him, and he sat up not quite knowing where he was. Mitch quickly looked around and noticed that the train was now packed with riders, many of whom had to stand because of the lack of available seating. As the train's warning broadcasted the doors closing, Mitch looked at the train car in front and noticed three men departing; two of the men looked to be North African and the other was a Caucasian with a limp. The darker complexed men made him edgy. *Stop it Mitch,* he scolded. *You're overreacting. They're probably just ordinary guys getting off work on their way home. Damn, the lady next to me stinks!*

The movement of the train made the limping man gaze in Mitch's direction. At that precise moment, their eyes met, the man with the limp immediately grabbed the arm of one of the North Africans while pointing at the window where Mitch was sitting. "HOLY SHIT ITS HUNT," Mitch screamed as he quickly stood and attempted to push the heavy woman off the seat. The lady yelled as he climbed over her and struggled to get past the passengers standing near the door. Unfortunately, the doors were firmly closed and all he could do was stare through the window. It was too late, and Mitch knew that the train would soon pass under the Potomac River before the next stop. By then Seth Hunt would have disappeared into the DC darkness.

Mitch stood stoically as his mind scrambled with questions. *Was I seeing things? What the hell is he doing here? Was it really him? There must be something that brought him to DC. I'm sure he wouldn't come all the way from Algeria just to try and kill me! What's with the limping?* He continued to stand at the door as the passengers moved around him getting off and on the train.

Mitch focused on his next move. *Shit! Who can I turn to for help? How can I convince the authorities that I just saw the leader of the largest and most dangerous Algerian terrorist organization walking the streets of DC? Besides, no one will believe me if I told them that Seth Hunt is linked to the al-Qaeda and Osama bin Laden. Should I tell the members of the investigation committee tomorrow that I saw*

Hunt, or keep my mouth shut? They'd probably think that I've really lost my mind. Damn them!

The cold night wind and snow blew against Mitch's face and snapped him out of his mental debate. He carefully walked to the stairs, but slipped on the wet steps as he worked his way down to the street level. Mitch hailed a cab. "I'm going to Christ Church." The trip took less than five minutes as the taxi pulled up outside of the old colonial church. Mitch handed the cabbie the fare, "Thanks buddy."

"I guess it's never too late to get right with the man upstairs."

Mitch laughed hearing the cabbie's remark. "Actually, I live across the street and down a side alley. It's just easier to get dropped off here because every cab driver knows Christ Church."

Mitch slowly walked in the cold dark night to his stable flat. He opened the unlocked door and felt just as cold inside as he did out in the ice and snow. *Damn it, I've gotta get the fire going and warm up this dump.*

Mitch threw a few small split logs that were stacked in a cardboard box into the fireplace and lit it. *That should do it!* But the fire despite numerous attempts didn't light. *Damn! Now there's smoke in the room.*

Mitch opened the door to rid the room of the foul odor then changed out of his uniform into something casual. He grabbed his parka and slammed the door shut. *What else can go wrong tonight? This whole situation pisses me off!*

Mitch quickly put his coat on and headed to Murph's Irish Pub for a quick bite to eat, stiff drink, and the warmth of their large fireplace.

8

The taxi pulled up to the Maghreb Merchant pottery shop in Alexandria. Abassi Sadi and Farid Benzai were waiting and quickly departed the shop and entered the taxi.

"Where to, fellas?"

"Take us to 3159 Row Street in Falls Church. It's the Dar Al-Hijrah Center."

"Okay. If I recall correctly isn't that the largest mosque in Virginia?" the cabbie asked as he drove to the DC Beltway and headed northwest to Falls Church.

"I'm not sure, but it is rather large for a mosque in America," Abassi replied and then looked at Farid. *"Il est de la merde."*

Farid laughed and whispered, "Yes, he is shit like all American infidels."

The cabbie looked up into his rearview mirror at the two men but said nothing. The beltway was congested with commuter traffic heading home for the evening, which delayed their arrival for evening prayer.

"Is there an alternate route you can take?" Abassi asked in frustration.

"Sorry, but this is the best and fastest way to go." The driver knew of alternate quicker routes. He had learned French from his Canadian grandmother many years ago and understood what Abassi had said. He didn't appreciate the slight, so he made sure that he took the slowest route to Falls Church during commute hours.

The cab pulled up into the parking lot of the mosque and the two North Africans departed. They knew that evening prayer had already begun. As they entered the mosque, removing their shoes, a man dressed in robes approached them.

"You are late, and he is not happy. Anticipate anger from our leader once I take you to him." The robed man squinted in disgust and turned entering a darkened hallway.

Abassi swallowed hard and felt a sick nervousness in his stomach. He realized that if there was to be punishment, he must take the brunt of it.

The three men approached a door at the end of the hall and the man in robes softly knocked. An angry voice from within yelled, "Enter!"

"Sir, they have finally arrived."

"That is obvious, Gafar, now get out and leave me with these two scums!"

Abassi quickly glanced around the room. The leader was lounging on pillows, sipping tea, and dressed in robes.

"You two will stand and listen. No words will come from your mouth unless I ask a question. I have brought you to America for several reasons. They are all extremely important to the success of our jihad against the United States. The first reason you are here is to protect me anytime I depart the mosque. Anytime or anywhere, you will accompany me and be my security as it was in Algeria and earlier today in Washington. That means that if I tell you to meet me at a location at a certain time you will arrive thirty minutes early. Do you understand that you failed me today by arriving late?"

Abassi and Farid knew that answering with an excuse was pointless. Abassi answered, "We are truly sorry, and it will never happen again."

The man rose and stood directly in front of Abassi. "Unfortunately, your statement is not worthy." As quickly as the man spoke those words, he withdrew a small double-edged stiletto and sliced open the entire length of Abassi's right nostril. Abassi screamed in agony as he clutched his face. Blood oozed through his fingers, down his mouth and throat, and pooled on the floor. Farid immediately stepped backward anticipating a similar punishment. The leader calmly turned and looked at Farid.

Without saying a word, he swiftly kicked him in the groin. Farid's ruptured testicles caused his eyes to protrude, his tongue to extend, and he doubled over into a fetal position falling to the floor. His head struck the white marble tiles, and he was unconscious. The leader looked at the two men and spat on them. He turned to the door and walked out.

Shortly thereafter a cleric, who had served as a medic for the al-Qaeda, entered with a surgical bag and began to assist Abassi. Once the wound was cleaned and stitched the cleric- medic covered it with a large gauze. Then he turned to help Farid. By this time Farid had regained consciousness but couldn't move from the floor.

"Listen very closely," the cleric-medic said. "Don't ever violate the desires of our leader.

This that you experienced was nothing. I have seen him kill for mistakes much less than what you two committed. Within the hour he will return to this room. You will have it clean and presentable for him. You will wait here, and do not depart for any reason. I have rags and water for you to clean the floor of blood and the bile that was expelled when your colleague collapsed."

Within the hour, as anticipated, the leader returned. He scornfully gazed at Abassi and saw Farid still strewn on the floor. "Your companion must stand in my presence."

Abassi reached down and pulled Farid to his feet. Farid grunted with pain and found it difficult to standup straight. The leader sat on the pillows and stared at them.

"I will continue with what I was saying earlier. You are here to protect me. You are here to carry out any orders that I command. You are here to kill Colonel Mitchell Ross who is currently residing in Alexandria. You will carry out these commands, but if you fail you will die. Do you understand?"

Abassi was reluctant to say anything, and he knew that under Farid's present condition no words would be coming from him. The leader slowly rose from his pillows. Abassi realized that he had to answer. "Yes sir, we understand completely," he said.

The leader again sat on the pillows and Abassi felt immediate relief.

"When we are outside of the mosque you will call me by my former Christian name, Seth Hunt. You will not call me *leader* or *sir* when addressing me in public. We will speak English, but if there is difficulty in communicating then we will default to French and finally to Arabic.

Do you understand what I have just said?"

"Yes sir, we completely understand," both responded.

"That is good! Now listen very carefully. Before arriving in America, I had directed elements of our organization to continuously observe Colonel Ross. Where he resides. What metro trains he takes. His usual walking routes. Where he normally goes for meals. Where he socializes and with whom. I can tell you at this very moment Colonel Ross is in a small Irish bar in Alexandria. I expect you two to complete my final command concerning the colonel. I want him dead, and I want that now so I can get on with more important business here in American.

Kill him tonight and return here tomorrow morning at nine with his bloodstained shirt. Now get out. I am tired of looking at you!"

Abassi put his arm around Farid's shoulder and helped him as they left the room. The cleric-medic was waiting in the hallway and examined them one last time before their departure from the mosque.

"In two weeks, I will remove the stitches. As for your colleague, he will feel much better in the morning. I have summoned a taxi for you, but before you leave take this note. It has the address of Colonel Ross's residence and the name of the Irish bar. You know what must be done. Take care of it in spite of your wounds." With that said the cleric handed Abassi the note and pointed to the exit doors.

Once outside in the cold darkness, Abassi noticed the headlights and exhaust of the waiting taxi. He and Farid immediately entered the car as the cabbie asked. "Where to Mack?" "An Irish bar in Alexandria. It's called Murph's."

9

"Well, well, it be me friend Mitch Ross returnin' to Murph's for a wee bit of liquid R-and- R," Sean Doran said as he noticed Mitch enter and move toward a stool at the end of the bar. "So lad, yah appear in need of a little fire in yah belly. Me thinks it be bourbon that yah desire." With that said he turned to the row of bourbon bottles. "Would there be any special one for yah?"

"No, just grab a cheap bottle. I have a gut feeling that I'll be unemployed in the not-too- distant future. I need to save every buck I have." Mitch felt the fog of doom slowly descend on his soul.

Sean served a healthy shot to Mitch then resumed drying a few beer glasses. "So it appears yah day be just another shit day. Yah know lad, when I have days like that it means a double glass of fire and a warm bowel of Irish stew. They make a good bowl here at Murph's. Now it not be anywhere near me mum's, but I tell yah it be the best this side of the Atlantic. I not be lying to yah my friend, and the first bowl be on me."

Sean quickly moved down the bar and whispered to a waitress. She disappeared in the kitchen. Meanwhile, Sean looked over at the minstrel and pointed to his right eye. The Irish singer picked up on the sign and then his guitar. Softly he began to sing.

"When Irish eyes are smilin', sure 'tis like the morn in spring. In the lilt of Irish laughter you can hear the angels sing . . ."

The waitress stepped out of the kitchen with a steaming bowl of stew, a wedge of homemade bread, and a thick cut of butter. Sean served it to Mitch.

"Aye lad, here be yah dinner and a grand dinner it be! Nothin' finer this side of Ireland. Enjoy!" Sean smiled and walked down the bar to refill a few pints for a couple that were talking softly and stealing a kiss between sips of beer.

Mitch noticed the lovers and thought of Abella. He wished she was sitting with him sharing the stew and sipping his bourbon. It pained him deeply thinking of how different life would be if she was again part of his. But unfortunately, Abella was only a memory.

"Lad, yah look a wee bit forlorn. Buck up, that stew will brighten even the legions of Satan himself. Talkin' bout Satan, I be readin' the Post today and I came upon an interestin' story. It be about yah, Mitch, and a congressional investigation. There be a grand picture of yah in yah uniform, quite impressive I might add! After readin' the article I did a wee bit of computer research about yah. Yah life has been a continuous adventure from what I could gather. Even now yah deal with those that are at the highest levels of the US government. But I be very much leery of them political types, my friend. They be only out for their own good, their bank accounts, and their re-elections. I don't trust any of them, and that be why I left Ireland."

Sean leaned over the bar and whispered so others wouldn't hear. "We both have a dark past. Mine be associated with the Irish Republican Army many years ago. Now I don't mention that to anyone so please, Mitch, keep it close to yah heart and not yah tongue. I was with the IRA for many a year and I fought the British in Northern Ireland. I had me reasons to fight and rid Ireland of British rule. But when peace was finally made there were a few members of the IRA that the British government wanted arrested for war crimes. I be one of them and knew that I could no longer stay in me beloved Ireland. I left it all behind includin' my lady. I'm hopin' that one day I will save enough and have her come to America. But for now, I keep a low profile and work here at Murph's. I hope yah understand that I fled because me government was not protectin' me. It appears your government be doing the same thing and turnin' its back on yah."

Mitch put a hand on Sean's shoulder. "Sean, your secret will forever be hidden within me. You can count on that!" Mitch lowered his hand and grabbed the glass of bourbon raising it in a toast.

"Thank yah Mitch, I knew I could trust yah especially after readin' the article in the *Post*. It be interestin' and a well-written piece that compliments you as a military officer. I chuckled once I finished readin' because the reporter has such an Irish name, Colleen Duffy. Aye, now it doesn't get any more Irish than that!"

Mitch had just taken a large mouth full of stew when Sean mentioned Colleen's name.

The stew exploded out of his mouth as he coughed.

"Be there a problem with what I just said, Mitch?"

"Sorry Sean, but the reporter's name caught me by surprise. I just met her today and plan to see her tomorrow morning over coffee before the hearings resume. She seems to be a very nice lady."

"Those type might be nice, but they are always lookin' for a scoop. Be careful what yah might say to that lass. I'm sure she went home and wrote that article after she got to know yah. As I said she be very complementary about yah, but that could change if yah tongue slips and yah tell her a secret or two."

Sean turned and moved down the bar where two men were sitting and requested coffee.

Not that it was out of the ordinary Sean thought, but usually coffee is ordered with a little whiskey. Sean served them and returned to Mitch's end of the bar.

"That be interestin.' Those two gents sit at an Irish bar and only order coffee. To each their own, but two men ordering a nonalcoholic beverage is a little out of the ordinary in this pub. Also, they don't appear to have had the best of days. One has a bandage on his face and the other seems to be in constant pain as he sits on his barstool."

Mitch casually looked up into the bar's mirror so as not to attract attention. Both men were locked in an intense conversation speaking French. "Sean," Mitch whispered while staring down at his glass of bourbon. "This is not good. Without a doubt those men are here to kill me. I saw them earlier today with the leader of one of the largest and most powerful terrorist organizations in all of North Africa."

"Well me friend, if they be lookin' for a fight let the Donnybrook begin here!"

"No Sean, there'll be no fighting here at Murph's. If you would be so kind as to distract those two, then I'll slip out the door and run to my flat."

"But yah'll be alone and I'm sure those boys know where yah live."

"Please, Sean, just do what I ask. The sooner I get out of here the better."

Sean nodded and then slowly picked up the carafe of coffee. He took one last look at Mitch and then casually walked over to the two men. Without saying a word he began to refill one of the coffee cups. As he poured, Sean tipped the decanter too far and the scalding hot liquid splashed on the bar and into the laps of the men. They screamed in pain and began to yell in Arabic. Mitch had already departed into the cold dark night and was well on his way to his flat.

10

"Lads, lads, I be terribly sorry for spillin' the coffee on yah. Here, take the towels and wipe off near the fireplace," Sean said with little or no sympathy for the two North Africans.

Abassi looked at Sean with disdain as he reached into his jacket for his stiletto. He glanced at the end of the bar where Mitch had been sitting. There was only an empty stool and a partially filled glass of bourbon. "*Yah kalb* you fucking dog!" Abassi yelled, turning toward Sean realizing that the spilling of the coffee was no accident. He pulled his knife from his jacket pocket and ran to the door pushing shocked patrons out of his way. Farid painfully limped as he attempted to follow Abassi out of Murph's.

As Farid stepped into the frigid night air a taxi abruptly slammed its breaks and the back door flung open. "*Yaallah*," Abassi screamed to Farid from the backseat of the cab. "Let's go," he commanded the driver as Farid struggled to get in. Abassi pushed the piece of paper with Mitch's address in the driver's face. "Take us there, now!"

Sean had quickly settled the clientele down inside Murph's with a round of whiskey shots and a loud rendition of the Irish folk song, "Seven Drunken Nights." He turned to his colleague behind the bar. "Colin, watch the bar for me. I'll be takin' a long smoke break."

Sean grabbed his coat from behind the bar and an eleven-inch billy club that he kept to control unruly drunks. He took the back door of the pub knowing that it would be a shorter run to Mitch's flat.

Mitch was running full out near Christ Church when a taxi came around from Camron to North Columbus Street. The vehicle came to an abrupt stop as Abassi threw a twenty at the driver and leaped from the cab. Farid struggled while attempting to keep up. Mitch saw the shadowy figure of Abassi in the cold moonless night as he rapidly approached. *Oh shit . . . God help me!* Mitch thought as he continued to run. Flying into his flat he slammed the door and began to stack and wedge anything that he could find against the entrance. He had no weapons to protect himself.

It was pitch black in his flat and he stumbled around while panic was overtaking his ability to reason as pounding and slamming from outside increased. Abassi was pushing and kicking at the old wooden door. With each impact the entrance opened a few more inches.

Mitch was forcing anything he could find against the door, but there seemed to be nothing left. He looked over his shoulder while still pushing on the door, there was an image of a man wearing an old military officer's uniform. The ghostly figure hovered and pointed to a battered wooden floor plank to the left of where Mitch was standing. The plank was sticking slightly out from the rest of the floor. Mitch grabbed the end of the plank pulling it up. He quickly turned and wedged it under the door, slowing Abassi's progress.

Mitch tripped and fell backward near the gaping hole in the floor while pushing the plank into place. Attempting to get up, his left arm slid into the gap and Mitch touched an oddly shaped metal object.

The pounding on the door increased and the plank shifted allowing Abassi to wedge his body between the opening of the door and the frame. Looking down in the darkness Mitch could barely make out an old metal chest. Opening it, he discovered a small flintlock pistol. As Mitch pulled it from the chest there was a crashing noise. He turned as Abassi leaped over the debris and flew at him. Mitch saw the glimmer of the knife and felt Abassi crash upon him on the floor near the fireplace. The terrorist quickly raised the stiletto, thrusting it at Mitch who felt the blade slice against his cheek and then warm blood rushed down his face and pool into his ear. He reached up with his left hand to prevent the downward fatal blow of the knife. Abassi was a larger stronger man and as much as Mitch struggled, the knife slowly moved closer to his chest. Abassi stared into Mitch's eyes and spat in his face. As the two men continued to struggle in their death grip the strange ghostly image reappeared for a fleeting moment and Mitch heard a voice.

"My flintlock . . . use it Colonel."

Mitch was still holding the ancient pistol and instantly raised it to Abassi's face and pulled the trigger. The weapon hesitated then a small spark appeared as the flint struck the metal fizzen and ignited the powder within the barrel. The pistol fired a flame followed by a small lead ball. The aged projectile crashed into Abassi's face at point-blank range, cracking his skull. His eyes opened wide and crossed as the knife fell from his hand and he rolled to the right lying dead next to Mitch.

Farid had finally entered the flat and raised his knife for the kill. Just before he could thrust it down, a silhouette violently hit Farid in the head. As Farid's lifeless body struck the floor, Mitch heard a familiar voice.

"Aye, me thinks that bastard will be going nowhere for a while. Hmmm . . . I haven't lost me touch with the old blackjack." Sean glanced at the club and then reached down to help Mitch get up. "That be a mean lookin' cut on yah face, Mitch. Let's get some water and wipe it clean."

"Sean you're a life saver! I was still dazed by the first terrorist and didn't see the second until he was almost on top of me."

"Mitch, I heard a gunshot just before enterin' your flat. It seems as though the man lying next to you took the shot in the face." Sean was looking down at Abassi when he noticed the metal chest. "Glory be in heavin'. I can't believe what me eyes are seein'. It be the chest of Major Phillips! Mitch, you found it! So, it not be an old wives' tale after all."

Mitch raised his right hand that still held the flintlock pistol. "Thank God. By some miracle it still had dry powder!"

"Now speak the truth to me, lad. Yah saw him didn't yah? Major Phillips, he be here with yah. Glory be . . . for over two hundred years he be waitin' to save yah life."

"Sean, I saw him, and he talked to me. Had it not been for the ghost of Major Philips I'd be dead."

"There be a lot of questions by the authorities when they arrive tonight. Explainin' that flintlock might be a wee bit difficult. Mitch, don't mention anythin' about Major Phillips. The coppers will think yah daft and gone mad if yah do. Just tell them yah collect old black powder weapons."

11

The next morning Mitch was up well before sunrise. He hadn't slept well, and his sliced cheek throbbed with each heartbeat. Sean and he had attempted to patch up the cut, but he felt awkward wearing the bandage. His flat was a complete disaster and the police had restricted Mitch from staying in the crime scene. Sean had convinced Mitch to spend the night at his small apartment, and the couch had been unbearable. But Mitch was thankful for Sean and his generosity.

Mitch dressed in his uniform and slipped out of the apartment walking to King Street metro station. It was still dark and cold as Mitch went up the escalator. He waited only a few minutes for the train and stepped into the nearest car. It was extremely crowded with rush hour commuters, and he had to stand the entire journey to L'Enfant Plaza station near Capitol Hill. As he left the station and pulled up the collar of his heavy military coat to ward off the icy wind he glanced at his watch. Mitch had thirty minutes to walk a ten-minute route to the coffee shop and hopefully meet Colleen.

As he approached the café he noticed the *Post* reporter inside sitting near the window. As she looked up and saw Mitch her demeanor rapidly changed from happiness to shock. She quickly approached Mitch, raising her hand and lightly touching the wound on his face.

"Mitch, a colleague of mine told me on the train this morning that he had heard of an attack and death in Alexandria. Now I see you've been hurt. Was it you who was attacked? Please tell me, I promise I won't write anything about it."

"Well, I was going to say that I cut myself shaving. But I suspect you being a reporter probably would hear about the attack before most folks. Yes, I believe two extremists had been out to kill me. One is dead and the other is in the hospital unconscious. But let's sit down and talk about something else."

Colleen turned and walked to the small table near the large window of the café. "Is this okay Mitch, or should we move to that booth near the wall?"

"Let's move to the booth. There are less people that'll notice my patched-up face."

They ordered coffee and talked about the snow that was beginning to fall. But Mitch could tell Colleen wanted to know more about the terrorists and how he knew they were out to kill him.

"Much of what you have heard in the hearings, and will hear, center on Captain Seth Hunt. He's an evil man who has turned his back on American, and I believe desires to destroy our way of life. Those two men that attacked me last night were bodyguards of Captain Hunt."

"How do you know that?"

"After leaving you in the gardens of the Capitol yesterday evening, I continued to the metro station. It was while riding the train that I saw Captain Hunt and the same two men walking through the Foggy Bottom station. They saw me, and I realized that it would be just a matter of time before they would attempt to kill me. As luck would have it, as the terrorists were breaking into my flat, I had a couple friends save my life."

"Why does Captain Hunt want to kill you?"

"Perhaps I shouldn't respond to your question, but at this point in my life I have nothing to lose. There are only a few that truly know the hatred that Captain Seth Hunt has for America. I unfortunately am one of those remaining few, and he wants me dead. Hunt was the individual who betrayed us during our rescue attempt in the Casbah. It was his jihadist terrorists that attacked and killed members of my rescue team. Over the decades of Hunt's captivity, by numerous terrorist organizations, he was converted to radical Islam, tested over the years to prove his allegiance to Osama bin Laden, brainwashed to believe that America is the great Satan and must be destroyed. Now he has become the leader of the largest Algerian terrorist organization affiliated with the al-Qaeda. His organization is known as the GSPC. I hope this answered your question."

"My God, you were so fortunate. Those friends of yours are they okay?"

"Yeah, they're just fine and I spent the night at the apartment of one of them."

"Please be more careful. I would hate to think that this would be the last time I would ever spend a private moment with you."

"Not to worry, I've been through much worse and something tells me that there'll be many more moments together." Mitch smiled at Colleen then motioned to the waitress for more coffee.

For the next hour they talked about everything other than the congressional hearings and the attack. At 8:20 they decided that it was time to depart for the Capitol building.

"Mitch, why don't you leave first, and I'll follow in ten minutes," Colleen said quietly while putting on her coat.

"Thanks for spending time with me this morning. It really helped me forget how screwed up my life has gotten. I'm sure most of those congressional folks in the hearing have already heard of the attack. I just want all of this to end, but I know it will continue on for the unforeseeable future. I'll look for you from time to time during the hearing today," Mitch said as he finished buttoning his coat and walked out of the café.

12

Mitch stood behind his chair in the congressional hearing room as Senator Levin called the room to order.

"Colonel Ross, I remind you that you're under oath. Before we resume questioning, I want to say that this senator and the members of the congressional hearing sincerely hope that you're feeling well. I was briefed on the attack just before I entered the room this morning. From my understanding, you are very fortunate to have only sustained the wound on your face.

"At this time the questioning will begin." Senator Levin looked at the green lights on the wall behind Mitch. But before recognizing anyone on the committee, he reached into his coat pocket and placed the president's note that he had received the day before next to his microphone. "I now recognize the honorable senator from the state of North Carolina, Daniel Hill."

"Thank you, Mr. Chairman." Senator Hill paused before speaking as he stared at the bandage on Mitch's face.

The silence in the room seemed to be deafening and Mitch could feel his hands shake. *Come on damn it! Don't let these guys get to you!*

"Colonel Ross, I served in Desert Storm and truly understand the great sacrifices that you made, especially during combat. Thank you for your service to our country. I was informed this morning by my staff about the attack you experienced. Thank goodness you survived.

Mr. Chairman, if I may I would like to ask Colonel Ross about the attack that occurred last night. I understand that this investigation is to probe into what happened and who was ultimately responsible for the failed attempt to rescue Captain Hunt. But I believe that what occurred last night is a consequence of the failed operation in the Casbah. What we might learn from last night's attack will help us determine more than just why this hearing came about."

"You may proceed with your questions, Senator Hill."

"Colonel Ross, those two men who attempted to kill you last night, do you have any idea who they are and whether they were affiliated with terrorist groups in Algeria?"

Damn it I'm under oath, how much should I divulge? If I disclose that I saw them with Hunt in a DC metro station, this hearing will explode into another chaotic moment and I'm sure he would be on the next flight out of here. I don't want that traitor to escape! I owe it to Dave McQueen to get that son of a bitch!

"Colonel Ross, do you need Senator Hill to restate his question?" Senator Levin interrupted.

"No Senator, I completely understand his question."

"Senator Hill, although my contact with those two men was fleeting, I believe they were North Africans. But I cannot say just based on their ethnicity whether they are or were affiliated with terrorist groups."

"Colonel, why do you speculate that they're North Africans?"

"Having lived in North Africa for many years I can distinguish those that are from that region. Especially those who live north of the Atlas Mountains along the Mediterranean Sea. The majority of countries in that region are former colonies of France. And I heard my two attackers speaking French."

"If they're North Africans and wanted to kill you, don't you think that they're Algerians affiliated with the terrorist group, GSPC? That would be the same organization that you fought in the Casbah. Isn't that correct, Colonel?"

Shit! He's painting me into a corner.

"Sir, as I stated before I believe they were North Africans. But specifically identifying them as Algerians is something that I can't verify. Therefore, I can't say in all honesty whether they are members of the GSPC. What I can tell you is those that I fought in the Casbah, while attempting to rescue Captain Hunt, were members of the GSPC."

"Colonel, now that you're back in the United States and most likely will never return to North Africa, why is it so important that extremists should target you? Is there something that you're aware of that you haven't disclosed? Remember you're under oath."

Damn his questions! I'm getting closer to that preverbal corner, and he has the paint brush. "Senator Hill, perhaps the attack that occurred last night was purely out of revenge for what had happened in Algeria. I'm just speculating at this point, but I can guarantee that I will not return to North Africa. Actually, I believe I possess no value for any radical extremist group."

"Colonel, contrary to what you might believe, I'm sure those extremists were ordered by a very powerful individual to take you out. Perhaps it was for revenge, but I'm certain it had to do with your actions in Algeria. I also believe that you hold critical information that they know would threaten their entire operation. Unfortunately, I just don't know exactly the question to ask. Mr. Chairman, I have no further questions."

Thank God! That senator was getting dangerously close to the truth.

The committee chairman glanced at the president's note next to his mic. "Thank you, Senator Hill. At this time I will recess this hearing and we will reconvene at two o'clock this afternoon. Colonel Ross, I need a moment with you."

Mitch was stunned by Senator Levin's request and immediately approached the chairman's dais. "Sir, you wanted to discuss something?"

"Colonel Ross, yesterday I received a note from President Bush.

He has requested your presence this morning in the Oval Office. You're to be there at eleven o'clock. I'm sure the meeting will not extend beyond an hour considering his daily schedule. As I stated, we will reconvene the hearing at two. Good luck Colonel." Senator Levin turned as his chief of staff approached with a concerned look and a handful of notes.

- • - •

"Mitch, you look dazed. Is everything okay?" Colleen had waited while he talked to Senator Levin.

Mitch looked up and smiled. "It never ends. Now the president wants to see me."

"The president of the United States? When? Why?"

"I've gotta leave now. I don't know why he wants to see me. How about if we meet in the same café at one this afternoon for a quick coffee."

"I'll be waiting for you inside." Colleen stared into Mitch's eyes worried that the outcome wouldn't be good.

Mitch grabbed a taxi and proceeded to the White House entry point. Once cleared by security he walked to a side access door and was greeted by another security agent and a White House staff member.

"Colonel Ross, welcome to the White House. You're a little early but that's good because there's a break in the president's schedule. He'll see you now. Please follow me." The young woman turned and walked down a broad hallway toward the Oval Office. She nodded at the president's secretary and then lightly tapped on the door and cracked it open.

"Mr. President, Colonel Ross is here to see you."

"Please have him come in, and Katherine, I can take it from here." She opened the door stepping to the side allowing Mitch to enter. "Come in Colonel and have a seat on the couch."

Mitch felt extremely awkward as the president walked around his desk. President Bush extended his hand and Mitch firmly gripped it.

"Now that's a good military handshake. You'd be surprised how many come in this office and give me a limp soft hand. I can generally judge a man by how he shakes my hand. In Texas you're taught from day-one how to give a good firm shake. Please sit and let's talk."

The president sat across from Mitch separated by a rectangular coffee table with a small basket of flowers.

"Colonel, I'm not going to waste your time or mine. I want to get straight to the point. There's a lot of congressional folks wrapped up in those hearings concentrating on the failed attempt to rescue Captain Seth Hunt. They should be spending their time working on the peoples' business of this great country. They shouldn't concern themselves with what happened in Algeria. I ordered that mission and I'm going to take full responsibility for it. Colonel, under the conditions that were levied on you, I believe that your planning, implementation, and performance were outstanding. I read your after-action report and that of the CIA operatives in Algeria. From what I could gather you did everything possible to get Hunt out of there. But that individual is what we call in Texas a turn coat, a traitor to the United States. It's extremely unfortunate that there were lives lost in the operation. I've personally contacted Chief Warrant

Officer David McQueen's parents with my condolences. I also had the deputy secretary of state travel to Algeria and represent the United States at the funerals of Djamila Belazzoug and her father."

Mitch flinched at hearing of the death of Djamila and her father. The president noted Mitch's reaction and immediately inquired if there was something wrong.

"Colonel Ross, were you not aware of the death of Djamila and her father?"

"Mr. President, I have been restricted of all communications and information concerning what happened in the Casbah after I lost consciousness. I was not aware that Djamila and her father were killed. It truly breaks my heart to know that they are no longer with us. She and her father were wonderful people and didn't hesitate to sacrifice all for me and America."

"I'm terribly sorry to hear that you weren't aware. This whole situation has resulted in such great tragedy and heartache." President Bush rose from the couch and walked to his desk.

Mitch had not anticipated the president's movement and felt embarrassed for not standing and showing respect.

"Colonel, I've thought about this since the word got to me that there would be a special congressional investigation about your actions in Algiers. As I said when you first came into the Oval Office, you did nothing wrong. You carried out my orders explicitly. Therefore, I'm sending a letter to the chairman of the Congressional Investigation Committee, Senator Levin. The letter states that I'm taking full responsibility for the actions that occurred in Algeria during the attempted rescue of Captain Seth Hunt. I have included the fact that you performed your duties magnificently during the operation and that I as the commander in chief request your continued service in the military without any blemish to your record. Also, I have recommended to Chairman Levin that the investigation cease immediately! If Congress demands that the hearings continue because they believe you are guilty, then I will checkmate them and grant you a full presidential pardon. I don't think it will come to that because Senator Levin is an intelligent man and knows that it would not be in his best political interest to defy my decision. Plus, from what I gather in the press you are becoming quite popular with the American people for showing grit and patriotism. Colonel, I'm aware of the attack that occurred last night. Your wound looks painful. You're very fortunate to have survived, and once the story hits the press it will endear you even more with the public."

President Bush signed the letter and walked back to the area where Mitch stood. "Colonel, I will have the letter delivered immediately to Senator Levin and copies will also be sent to the secretaries of Defense, the Air Force, and the director of the Defense Intelligence Agency. I wish you well and hope that you will continue your outstanding service to our country."

Mitch stood and the president patted him on the shoulder then shook his hand.

"Thank you, Mr. President. Your words are extremely complementary, and I'm humbled by your kindness. I entered the Oval Office thinking that my career had ended, but now I depart knowing that I will continue to proudly serve America. I'm emotionally overwhelmed by all that has just occurred."

"To help you remember this day, take the pen that I used to sign the letter. The pen itself is insignificant, but what it represents holds the true value of its worth. Thank you again, Colonel." The president turned and walked to his desk as Mitch left the Oval Office still attempting to comprehend all that had just occurred.

Katherine was waiting near the president's secretary and nodded at Mitch as she proceeded down the long hallway. "Please follow me, Colonel."

They walked in silence until they got to the door that would lead Mitch outside of the White House. "I hope that your visit with the president was worthwhile. I must be honest with you Colonel, when you arrived you seemed to be ill. But now there is an obvious spring to your step. Have a great day."

"Thank you. Yes, it's a fantastic day!"

13

There was a slight breeze off the sea as two women stood looking out at a fishing boat slowly returning with its catch. Sea gulls swooped and screeched behind the boat as they battled for remnants of fish that the sailors slowly dumped into the water. The sun was fading and spraying its last brilliant reddish glow over Notre Dame d'Afrique.

"My little lamb, this has always been my favorite spot to stand and lookout over the beautiful sea. Truly God is the greatest artist of all. The colors, the breeze, the freshness of the air. Yes, life is truly a gift." Mother Superior smiled warmly and then became more solemn.

"Each time we are here I feel your sadness. I don't understand why? You should have the glow of God's love burning within your heart and soul. Without a doubt you are the most exceptional novice I have ever had the privilege to lead on the journey to become a nun. Every task that you have been given is completed magnificently with maturity, intelligence, and passion. But yet I sense a reluctance when there is talk of the final vows. It's not uncommon to feel an unwillingness as you step closer to committing your life to the church and giving your heart to God. Even I as a young woman had those thoughts, but now I'm so grateful for the life God has given me.

"We have talked, the archbishop and I, about your future. We both feel that once you take your final vows your path should begin at the Vatican. The Holy Father knows of your outstanding abilities and desires that you spend your first two to three years in Rome. I have never known a young nun given such an opportunity. Truly God has blessed you. Perhaps I have told you too much and should let the archbishop explain. He holds much more information than I. But I wanted to be the first to tell you of the gift from the Holy Father."

"Mother Superior, I'm overwhelmed by the generosity of the church, the Holy Father, and God. Yes, I'm truly blessed. But there is so much that I must consider. My life is complicated and only God and time will help me understand my path. You have been very kind, and I will never be able to repay you for all your love and caring."

"Again, I see great sadness in your heart. There is something that weighs heavily on your soul. Talk to God and have him help you. But now my lamb, we must return to the Basilica. The sun is setting and the archbishop requests your presence."

The two women turned from the sea as the sun disappeared below the horizon and the breeze cooled. They quietly entered the Basilica and walked to the archbishop's office.

"Please enter." The archbishop said as Mother Superior lightly touched Abella's hand, opened the door, and then walked away after softly closing the portal.

Abella noticed the sad tired look on the old man's face as he stared at her while she bowed in his presence. The archbishop had always been a part of her life, but this evening he knew would be the last he would ever sit and talk with her.

"Please my little one, sit and let me look at you and say a few words. You are at life's crossroads and must decide. So few people in this world have such opportunities. Depending on your decision, will define the rest of your life. God and the church have offered you what others are never given. But yet in a few moments there will be a knock at my door. The messenger will offer you a completely different life. I cannot and will not pressure you one way or the other. Only you and God will determine your path. But if there ever becomes a time when you realize that you have taken the wrong path, there's no harm in turning around and walking the other way."

The archbishop slowly stood as if he had heard a fateful knock at his door. He seemed solemn and weary as he softly placed his hand on Abella's bowed head and prayed quietly in Latin. A tear streaked down his cheek as he waited for the inevitable. Mother Superior was standing at the door in front of someone hidden in the shadows of the darkened hallway.

"Father, he has arrived."

With a saddened sigh the archbishop stepped back and said, "Please have him enter."

Slowly Mother Superior stepped aside and allowed the tall shadowy figure to enter the room. As the weak light of the office flickered and cast its rays on the individual, Abella instinctively looked up. She froze, struggling to breathe as the stranger slowly turned and stared at her.

- • - •

Forgetting all protocol, Abella leaped from her chair and wrapped her arms around the tall slim man who was wearing a French military officer's uniform.

"Yves, Yves you've come back as you promised. It's been so long since I last saw you. I thought perhaps you had given up on me and forgotten all that I had hoped for." Abella cried as she held Yves tightly and buried her head in his chest.

The archbishop slowly and with gloom walked behind his desk and slumped in his chair.

There was an air of defeat as that of a prizefighter that had just taken a beating.

Abella glanced at the elderly man and realized that her actions and spoken words had hurt him greatly. During her life's trials and tribulations, he had always been there for her. He had been her rock throughout it all and now she was turning away.

"I'm so sorry, Father. Please forgive me! I love the church and all that you have given me during my life. But my heart cries for someone else. It would not be right for me to continue on this path with the church. If I did, I would be a hypocrite and God would never forgive me. Please understand! It seems as if a lifetime has passed since I last saw Colonel Dureau. He is my link to what my heart cries and yearns for. I pray that he has brought me the news I so long desire." Abella wiped her tears as she looked up at Yves. He smiled, noticing the dark drab color of her habit.

"Abella, even though there is little light in this room and your gown isn't a Versace, I had forgotten what a beautiful flower you are. But now let me explain to you where we are and why it has taken so long. I have your new passport in my pocket if you still desire to use it. It's a French passport, and if you take it, you are no longer Algerian. Perhaps at this moment you should not ask why or how it was obtained, but you are very fortunate to have received it. Had it not been for the influence of the archbishop and the Vatican, I'm sure that it would never have come to pass. There are no longer falsehoods in your record that linked you to the al-Qaeda's Algerian GSPC terrorist group. Those lies that prevented you from departing Algeria are no longer a factor. Your record is clean. Please don't question how it was accomplished or why you must be of French nationality and not Algerian. It is your ticket to Paris, which is your new home, if that is what you want. From there we will work on getting you to America."

Abella felt faint as she firmly held on to Yves' arm attempting to comprehend what she had just heard. *This can't be true.* She thought while looking at the archbishop and then back to Yves.

"Is this a dream?" she said through her tears. "Have my prayers finally been answered?"

"Yes my lamb, it's all true. If you still desire to leave the church I understand. But I must be completely honest with you, it breaks my heart knowing that you will never return. I christened you as a newborn here in the Basilica of Notre Dame d'Afrique. I knew your mother well. I truly felt when you lost your parents that God had appointed me to watch over you. But alas, you have grown into a beautiful intelligent woman who no longer needs my protection. I will pray for you each day that I remain on the earth. God bless you my little one." The archbishop sat sadly behind his desk as the tears streaked down his face.

- • - •

"With all due respect, sir, I would like to talk to Abella outside of your office," Yves said with a tone of sympathy and reverence.

"That won't be necessary, Colonel, I'm late making my rounds this evening. Use my office as I know you have much to discuss." The archbishop slowly moved toward the door, briefly pausing near Abella and lightly touching her face before departing.

Once alone in the office, Yves pulled the French passport from his coat pocket and handed it to Abella.

"We have much to discuss and so little time. You only have tonight and a few hours in the morning to say goodbye to all your friends and love ones here at the Basilica. Your flight to Paris departs tomorrow morning at ten. You need only to take what clothes you have that will fill one suitcase. I can't overemphasize the fact that you are no longer Algerian. Please make that mental transition so that there will be minimal issues when clearing customs here in Algeria and at Charles de Gaulle Airport in Paris."

Yves reached into the inner pocket of his uniform and pulled a small folded white card. Written on the inside were two sets of numbers and an address. "Abella, please safeguard this card because it not only contains your Paris address, but also cipher lock combinations. The combinations allow you to enter the outer gate of the apartment complex and permit you to enter my apartment, which is near Passy metro station. Also, I have an envelope for you."

Yves pulled an executive-sized envelope from a large outer pocket of his coat and handed it to Abella.

"Take this, it contains enough Euros for you to use while staying in Paris. If you find that you need more, I've left another envelope in my apartment. It's on a shelf within a book entitled *Vincent Van Gogh*. Now don't forget, I'll be waiting outside the Basilica in my Peugeot at eight tomorrow morning to take you to the airport. I know that all of this must be quite overwhelming for you, but we are on a very narrow timeline and for your safety you must depart as soon as possible. French intelligence at the embassy informed me that the GSPC had recently discovered that you were here in the Basilica. Their noose is rapidly tightening, and their goal is to capture and kill you. So we have to get you out of this country no later than tomorrow morning! Do you have any questions?"

"Yves, how can I ever repay you for all that you have done? It's exactly as you had promised, but I do have one question. Have you heard from Mitch? Where exactly is he and how is he doing? I hope and pray he still wants me as much as I miss and want him."

"Abella, all I know about Mitch is what the French Embassy in Washington has told me. He is currently under a congressional investigation. I've been told that he is restricted in where he goes and who he communicates with. Therefore, it doesn't surprise me that I've heard nothing from him. I'm sure he misses you greatly. One of the agents at the embassy mentioned that there was an article in the *Washington Post* about Mitch. Something about how he is not letting the congressional representatives belittle him in the investigation. The agent seemed to be quite impressed with Mitch."

"Hopefully by the time I get to DC all of the investigations will be over. Then Mitch and I can get back to planning our future together. But in the meantime, I've got to say goodbye to many wonderful people and leave my country forever. Algeria holds countless memories, and tomorrow will be a very difficult emotional day for me. But I understand that at the airport I must maintain and think of my future. I can't breakdown while clearing customs or else I may jeopardize my departure to Paris. I'm sure there are GSPC members lurking about in the airport, so I must be strong."

14

The taxi pulled up along the curb outside of the café where Colleen anxiously awaited. Mitch paid the driver and practically sprinted into the restaurant. Colleen had secured the same booth that they had earlier in the morning to maintain their privacy. As Mitch looked around the crowded café, Colleen stood and waved. There was definitely a change in Mitch's demeanor as he didn't care who was in the café that might recognize the two of them.

"Mitch, I love to see that smile, although the bandage covers half of your mouth." Colleen laughed. There was a positive glow about Mitch that she had never seen. "Tell me what happened in the White House. I can't stand the suspense!"

"I went into the Oval Office and sat with the president. It was brief but beyond anything that I could've imagined. Colleen, he's taking full responsibility for all that happened during the rescue attempt. He signed a letter which was sent to Senator Levin, the secretaries of Defense and the Air Force, and the director of the Defense Intelligence Agency. The letter requests that my military record be cleaned of any references to the failures in the Casbah. I'm to continue in my career as an Air Force colonel. My head is still spinning from all that's happened today."

"Oh Mitch, I'm so happy for you!" Coleen leaned over the table and softly kissed Mitch, immediately feeling the flush of embarrassment engulf her entire face. "Damn, I hope I didn't step over the line."

Mitch laughed as he reached out and held her hand. "Not at all. Actually, it was very sweet of you. But to tell you the truth, I'm not completely exonerated. The committee must decide whether to continue or drop all the charges against me. That will probably take a special vote. The president said that if the committee continues down the road to find me guilty, then his plan is to use a pardon."

"Wow, this is fantastic news. Mitch, if you don't have any reservations can I write an article about your visit with the president. I won't get into great detail, but the American people need to know what type of a leader he is. In this day and age of mud-slinging politics, it's refreshing to know that we still have a few leaders who refuse to throw people under the bus just to protect their own agendas."

"I like the way you think." Mitch said as he smiled at Colleen and squeezed her hand. He glanced at his watch. He had just under an hour before returning to the hearing room.

15

Senator Levin opened a folder that he had carefully placed on the table prior to the commencement of the hearing. The room was silent as Levin quietly reread the letter that was in the folder. He removed his glasses and slowly sat up in his chair. He cleared his throat and spoke.

"At noon, I received a letter from the president. He has made it abundantly clear that he is taking full responsibility for the failure of the attempted rescue of Captain Seth Hunt. He has requested that Colonel Ross be exonerated of all guilt and that his record remain unblemished as it was prior to the operation. The president has recommended that this investigation cease immediately."

Upon hearing the final statement there was an outburst of protest. Within moments the chairman stood and began to pound the table with his gavel. "This committee will come to order immediately! I will not allow this to go on! If this bedlam persists, then I will have no other recourse but to have the sergeant of arms remove those members who are out of order!"

The sergeant of arms rose from his chair and walked toward Senator Levin. Within a few minutes the room was quiet but tense. Levin looked around the room ensuring all members of the committee were ready to proceed.

"We will now take a vote to determine whether this investigation will continue or immediately cease as the president desires. I will address each member of the committee who will then respond verbally. A yea vote is to continue the investigation. A nay indicates a vote to cease the investigation. Does everyone understand the voting rules? The sergeant of arms will tally the votes and present the final count to me for the record. I will then announce the official results.

"I must stress to all members of this committee that the American people are quite aware of what has transpired thus far in these proceedings. I want each of you to think long and hard about how your vote will impact the outcome of these hearings and your political futures."

Each committee member was called upon to vote as Mitch sat stoically at his isolated desk, his thoughts drifting back to the final moments in the Casbah as Djamila attempted to keep Dave McQueen alive. He felt a deep sorrow knowing that Djamila and Dave had finally found each other, but their love was to end violently in a hail of terrorist bullets. Mitch glanced over his shoulder and noticed Colleen staring at him. She faintly smiled as she was recording the votes, noting that the count was very close.

After the final vote was cast, Chairman Levin nodded at the sergeant of arms who delivered the tally sheet. Levin scanned the tabulation and repositioned his microphone. A few members of the committee began to whisper and compare notes. Senator Levin looked again at the sheet given to him by the sergeant of arms.

"I have just received the final vote. I'm sure many of you know the outcome, but for the record I will announce the final accounting."

Levin paused, knowing that defying the president's wishes would damage his own political fortunes. The press would have a field day slamming Levin and the committee convicting an innocent man, a decorated hero exonerated by the president himself.

Levin nervously cleared his throat. "There were fourteen yea votes to continue the investigation and fourteen nay votes to immediately dismiss the hearings." Senator Levin paused to take a sip of water, then continued. "The rules established by this investigation committee state that in the event of a tie, the chairman would have the final deciding vote."

Immediately all whispering in the room ceased. Even the reporters stopped taking notes and waited for the final verdict.

16

"*Assalam alaikum,* Rabah. It is good to see you. I've worried about you since learning of the deaths of our beloved brethren at the hands of Colonel Mitchell Ross. It is my understanding from what has been whispered that you've replaced Abassi Sadi and Farid Benzai. That is not good news considering that Ahmad Muhammad is a madman. He cares for no one but himself and his fanatical ideals. I fear that all will eventually die who associate with him."

Rabah heard screaming in the distance, the sound echoing off the walls of the Al-Hijrah Mosque in Falls Church, Virginia.

"You can hear him screaming and cursing the failures of Abassi and Farid," the man said to Rabah. "It is said that Ahmad Muhammad, until this past year, had never tasted failure since becoming a Muslim. Since Colonel Ross appeared in his life, failure and disappointment have closely followed. Be very careful, my friend, I'm not sure who might be your worst enemy, Ross or Ahmad Muhammad. Even now Ahmad Muhammad, or as he desires here in America the infidel name Seth Hunt, shrieks and carries on as a wild animal caged and craving to kill. I foretell that the failure to kill Colonel Ross will directly impact the fulfillment of Hunt's al-Qaeda mission in America."

The two men abruptly stopped talking as angered screaming surged from the adjacent room of the mosque.

Although he was alone, Seth Hunt's loud piercing cries echoed throughout the mosque's hallways. "Those imbeciles failed me and may they burn in hell. It seems that I will be the only one that can kill Ross. I vow to Allah that Ross will be dead before weeks end! I have eyes that see his every move. Yes, he will die very soon."

"Rabah, if there is opportunity for you to distance yourself from this madman, Seth Hunt, please I beg you to disappear from his world. He has become heartless, and I feel that even Allah has turned away from him. His fanatical ideals will stop at nothing to destroy the world of the American infidels."

As the two men began to walk away from the piercing shrill of anger, Seth Hunt, yelled for Rabah.

"Rabah, I know you're in the hallway. Enter my room immediately! We must overcome our setbacks and annihilate the infidels to fulfill our jihad. Come quick or you will be punished as I have punished others that disobey me!"

Rabah reached out and hugged his companion while whispering. "Please pray that my soul will be with Allah if I'm not to survive this week."

— • — •

Rabah cautiously entered the dimly lit room anticipating a crazed man pacing like a demented trapped panther. But rather, what he saw was the opposite. Seth Hunt was calmly sipping tea and lounging on pillows in the corner of the bland darkened room. The only light came from a candle that burned near Hunt.

"Come, relax with me, Rabah, and have tea." Hunt casually said as he poured tea into a small glass cup.

Rabah nervously approached and sat on the pillows. His conspicuous shaking almost spilled the hot liquid as he took the cup. Then bowed his head in respect knowing the power that Hunt possessed as the leader of the Algerian GSPC terrorist organization.

"We will drink our tea and talk of life. Then, once we are finished, we will drive to Alexandria. Allah has informed me that it will be a beautiful evening. Yes, it will be exquisite watching Satan's infidel die. We will wait near the residence of Colonel Ross and once he appears we will kill him."

Hunt casually smiled and stared at Rabah with the deranged expression of a madman. Then he continued. "Allah has blessed me with a dream of pulling the trigger and purging the world of that cancerous scum."

Rabah attempted to hide his uneasiness, but his shaking caused the tea to spill. Hunt slowly set his cup near the burning candle, reached into his robe, and quickly pulled out an ancient Arabic curved dagger. Rabah attempted to move away, but Hunt was on him like a leopard attacking his prey. The knife swiftly made a surface cut on Rabah's throat, spilling his blood.

"There will not be any mishaps tonight. Do you understand! If I detect that you are weak, I will kill you as I plan to kill Colonel Ross," Hunt whispered as he continued to hold the knife against Rabah's throat.

Rabah was violently shaking, causing the dagger to saw deeper into his neck. "Please, I will obey all of your commands. Please, please spare my life, I have a wife and two children."

"Perhaps you should think of your family before you open your mouth." Hunt yelled.

Then he slowly lowered the dagger and viciously pushed Rabah toward the door. "Get out of my sight and in one hour we will depart for Alexandria."

Rabah, while clutching his bloody throat, stumbled out of the room. A cleric standing in the hallway stood wide-eyed..

"Please help me! I must run from here." Rabah whispered.

The cleric, standing in his white robe, grabbed Rabah by the arms and stared deep into his eyes. "I'm sorry, but you cannot leave. Ahmad Muhammad has made it abundantly clear to all those supporting his jihad that you have now been chosen to assist him. It is unwise to disobey his desires." The cleric led Rabah into a large room that had many basins of water and towels for all those needing to wash before the call to prayer. "Are you saying that there is no way out for me? What if I overpower you and run from here."

The cleric shook his head as he laughed. "If you attempt to leave without Ahmad Muhammad's consent, you and your family will be killed. It is as simple as that my Islamic brother."

Rabah slowly lowered himself into a wooden chair adjacent to a few basins of water. He slouched and placed his face into his palms and began to weep. He realized there was no escape from this nightmare.

17

"I as the chairman of this esteemed committee, after considering all that has been deliberated cast my vote . . ." Senator Levin, understanding the gravity of his decision, took a deep breathe while staring at the president's letter then at the members of the committee. "My vote is nay, and this investigation hearing is now officially closed! Colonel Ross, you are excused."

Immediately there was an uproar of voices and protests. Congressional interns and aides dashed about the room taking scribbled notes from their respective senators and representatives. Many of the reporters rushed from the room to call their news agencies to report the outcome. For the third time, the investigation committee had turned into uncontrollable chaos. But unlike the previous occurrences, Senator Levin didn't touch the gavel. He glanced at Mitch, who was now standing and nodding favorably as he walked out of the room.

"Mitch, Mitch it's over! You've won!" Colleen yelled above the bedlam as reporters elbowed her out of the way to get an exclusive interview.

Colleen stumbled and almost fell while the others rushed toward Mitch. He leaned into them, ignoring their questions, and reached through their microphones, taking Colleen's hand. Mitch gently pulled her toward him and headed for an exit door. Once clear of all the others, and finding an isolated location outside, he hugged her tightly.

"Thanks for being so kind and understanding during these damnable hearings. You truly helped me escape the pressure and strain, but it's not over. I haven't won until I find and stop Seth Hunt! Why he's here in DC is still a mystery to me. I know deep in my gut his presence doesn't bode well for America. I'll track that bastard down to the ends of the earth to make him pay for the deaths of those that were near to me in Algeria."

Colleen looked up while still being held by Mitch and lightly touched the bandage that was now bloodstained. "Mitch, your face seems swollen and bleeding. You need to have a doctor look at that. It's infected and causing your left eye to partially close."

"In all the excitement today I really hadn't noticed, but now that you mention it there is a lot of pain. I'll arrange something tomorrow. It's getting too late now."

"No Mitch, you've gotta go now. Isn't there a military hospital nearby?"

"Walter Reed is probably the closest. It's only about six miles from the White House."

"Okay we need to go now!" Colleen insisted as she pulled Mitch toward the steps of the Capitol.

"Whoa, what's this *we*, Kemosabe? Are you planning to accompany me?"

"Without a doubt! I know that once you're out of my sight you'll change your mind and not go to the hospital. By the way, who the hell is *Kemosabe?*" Colleen asked while still pulling Mitch closer to the steps.

"Okay, okay. I must get my coat and the paperwork that I left on the desk. Plus, I'm sure your things are in the hearing room along with your overcoat."

"Your right, but we're leaving immediately to the hospital after we get our belongings."

"Damn, once you make your mind up there's no turning back.

But I know it's for my own good so let's get going."

- • - •

They grabbed a taxi and within fifteen minutes entered the main doors of Walter Reed Army Medical Center. As they walked through the crowded lobby Colleen was looking for the emergency ward as Mitch inquired at the registration desk.

"Excuse me, where would someone go if they had a medical situation, but it wasn't critical?"

The receptionist looked at Mitch's bandaged swollen face, "Sir, you really need to be seen by a doctor. Please walk down aisle three, on your right, and report to the technician at the end of the hall. I'll call to let him know you're on your way. By the way, aren't you Colonel Ross that I've been reading about in the *Post*? A group of us here at the hospital think that you're quite the hero to standup to those politicians."

"Thank you for the kind words. Now you said it was aisle three?"

"Yes, just to the end of the hallway." The young receptionist smiled starry-eyed as if Mitch was a Hollywood star.

"Looks like you have a fan?" Colleen said while trying to suppress her laughter.

"Well, if it hadn't been for a reporter named Colleen Duffy and her *Post* articles, I would still be Colonel Joe Bag O'Donuts."

"What? You know it really amazes me the names you military folks come up with. Who the hell is Joe Bag O'Donuts?"

"I'll tell you later, Tonto, but first let me talk to this technician."

"*Tonto?*" Colleen rolled her eyes and laughed.

- • - •

As Mitch caught the attention of the technician, Colleen sat in the waiting area. "I'm Colonel Ross, the receptionist told me to see you."

"Yes sir, just got off the phone with her. That swelling doesn't look good, but once we get control of it the scar will complement the others on your face." The technician smiled but Mitch saw little humor in his statement.

"Is the doctor available?"

"Sorry Colonel, hope I didn't insult you. Yes, the doctor can see you now. His office is three doors down on the left." Mitch lightly knocked and entered.

"Colonel Ross, it's a pleasure to meet you. I've been keeping up with the newspaper reports of the investigation. It's great how you stick it to those folks on Capitol Hill. But I know you're not here to talk about the hearings. Let me look at that cut. Don't worry, I'll be careful removing the bandage."

The doctor closely examined the facial wound pushing on swollen areas which emitted a pus-filled blood mixture.

"Colonel, your wound is infected. Had it gone one more day your left eye would have been swollen shut. What I recommend is a high dose of antibiotics. We need to knock that infection out quickly." The doctor turned to his desk and scribbled illegible words on a prescription pad. "Take this to the pharmacy in aisle two. Good luck, Colonel, and keep giving those political blowhards hell."

"How did it go?" Coleen asked when Mitch returned.

"I've gotta pick up antibiotics at the pharmacy here in the hospital. Okay, let's get going before they close for the night."

Just before they entered the pharmacy Mitch heard something that made him abruptly stop. His head snapped to the right as he stared at a closed door.

"Mitch, is everything okay?" Colleen asked.

"Wow, that was odd. I could have sworn that I heard the voice of an old friend." As they both paused a Southern-accented voice drifted slowly from behind the door.

"Y'all have been very sweet to me during this long period of my convalescence. I do declare that at this point in my recovery there are only two thangs that can please this old man. Ifin' you had a rich tastin' Cuban Cohiba and a nice smooth glass of Kentucky magic my day would be complete. Now, don't shake that pretty head of yours ifin' you've never tried those gifts from God."

Mitch looked at Colleen and grabbed the door handle.

"Mitch, what are you doing? You can't just barge into a hospital room!" Colleen huffed, attempting to pull Mitch's hand from the door.

As Mitch swung the door open the unsuspecting nurse looked up in shock. The old man casually glanced over shaking his head accompanied by a large smile.

"Glory be in Heaven. I can't believe what my eyes are tellin' me." With that said he rose from his chair like a huge grizzly and engulfed Mitch in a bear hug. His size dwarfed everyone, but despite his mass the two men hugged as two lost brothers that had finally found each other.

"Colonel, you're a sight for sore eyes! I'm truly blessed today. Checkin' out of the hospital and seeing someone that I thought perhaps was either six feet under or on the other side of the world. But that patch on yah face tells me you've not journeyed far from trouble."

The nurse and Colleen stood astonished as they watched the two men hug, laugh, and cry.

Mitch finally broke free of his friend's strong grasp. "My God, I've found you, Jake, and you're alive! I had been told that you survived the terrorist attack but considering your condition it was hard for me to believe it."

"The last time I remember being with you, Colonel, you were cradling my head while fightin' terrorists in the Casbah. I knew it was you, but I couldn't see or speak. Then I heard that terrorist screamin' and I believe you were cracked upside the head. I don't remember anything after that until I woke up in a hospital.

Colleen finally began to put the pieces of the puzzle together. "Wait a minute, is this THE Jake Davis?"

Mitch turned toward her with tears and a broad smile. "Yes, this is the one and only. The man that saved my tail on many occasions in Algeria. He's truly the brother that I never had."

"It's almost as though I know you. What I've read and heard about you is amazing. Talk about a trailblazer." Colleen said while reaching out and shaking Jake's enormous, dark hand.

"Well little lady those are kind words, but I must say that the Colonel is quite the man himself. On two occasions that come to mind, had it not been for him, I'd be sittin' next to Gabriel playin' tunes in paradise." Jake grinned as the others began to laugh.

"Jake, gotta run to the pharmacy. But would there be any chance of linking up with you in the next few days? Maybe we can go for a nice steak and a little JB Black Label. I've got a place in mind that's along the Potomac in Alexandria. Maybe I can persuade Colleen to accompany us." Mitch glanced at Colleen.

"I don't know about Jake's schedule, but you don't have to ask me twice. I'd love to go and listen to all your Algerian adventures. Promise I won't take any notes." Colleen said with a chuckle.

"Colonel, that sounds like a great plan! I'll be lookin' forward to receivin' your call. By the way, nice meetin' yah young lady." Jake took a pen from the nurse's desk and a scrap of paper. He jotted down a number and handed it to Mitch.

Mitch grabbed Jake's meaty hand and attempted to shake it. "*Adios* my brother."

18

An overcast sky hung low along the Algiers coastal cliffs of the Mediterranean Sea. It was unusually dark and cool for that time of the morning.

Yves was getting nervous waiting in his car outside the Catholic Basilica. It was 8:10 am and the plan was for Abella to depart for the airport at eight. He was aware that the longer he waited the larger a target he became for GSPC terrorists who undoubtedly were surveilling the sanctuary. Yves also knew that Abella could not linger in the airport for fear of being abducted. Timing for her pickup and subsequent drop off at the airport was critical. So, he quickly left his car and ran up the steps to the entrance of the Basilica. He pulled on the oversized handle of one of the ancient wooden doors, which slowly opened. Looking around in the darkened interior he noticed the silhouette of a young woman crying.

"Abella, we must be going," Yves said firmly while she hugged Mother Superior and kissed the hand of the archbishop. Reality had finally set in and Abella realized that she would never again return to the Basilica. She wiped her tears, grabbed her well-worn brown leather bag, turned, and walked to the doors without saying another word. She understood the potential dangers that lurked beyond the protection of the Basilica. As Yves opened the large wooden door Abella lowered her head, tightly gripped her bag, and ran to Yves's

Peugeot. Yves slid behind the steering wheel, quickly started the car, and headed in the direction of the airport.

"We're a little behind our timeline, Abella, so let's hope there isn't much traffic on the road," Yves said in English as he aggressively accelerated while merging onto the main coastal road heading east. "I believe it would be better that we speak English and not French. I'm sure English was not spoken during most of the time spent in the Basilica. It's good for you to practice and prepare for your transition to America."

Abella gazed at the white French style nineteenth century buildings of Algiers that had been constructed during the height of the colonial era. She looked upon their beauty realizing that she would never see them again. The bay and harbor area of the city was slowly awakening to the large commercial shipping activities. Sea gulls clustered near the fleet of fishing boats that were returning with their early catch of the day. There was the scent of freshness in the morning air as the breeze entered the car through Abella's opened window. She was beginning to feel calm and relaxed until Yves abruptly changed lanes.

"Don't turn to look, but there's a black sedan that's been trailing us since we entered this main road."

"But Yves, there's a lot of cars on this route heading east. Why do you suspect the sedan is following us?"

"Each time I've accelerated, slowed down, and changed lanes other cars have passed except for the black Mercedes. It's maintained position behind us., Yves responded while looking into the rearview mirror.

Abella looked into the outside door mirror and noticed the sedan had positioned itself on the right shoulder of the road. "That Mercedes is accelerating on our right side. Yves, we've gotta move to the far-left lane . . . now!"

"I can't do that! There's a large truck blocking that lane. Hold on, I'm going to speed up and try to get in front of the truck."

Abella grabbed the door handle anticipating the acceleration of the Peugeot. But before Yves could stomp on the gas pedal there was a sickening impact from the right rear side of the car causing it to fishtail and skid. Yves desperately fought to keep control and avoid a collision with the large truck on the left. Abella quickly looked to her right and braced for another impact. But as the black Mercedes repositioned itself on the right, the passenger window opened, and a man with a large handgun took careful aim and fired. Abella ducked as she saw the flash of the discharging pistol.

"Ahhh!" Yves yelled then slumped over the steering wheel.

As the Peugeot went out of control, Abella seized the wheel with her right hand while attempting to pull Yves back against the seat with her left. His foot was still braced against the accelerator as the car's speed continued to increase.

"Yves, Yves . . . please help me!" she screamed as the black Mercedes repositioned for another shot. Abella turned the steering wheel violently to her right, which caused the Peugeot to slam into the Mercedes. The black sedan fell back a few feet and jolted Yves into an unsteady consciousness.

"Abella, I'm . . . hit. Maybe I can steer . . . with my right hand. Open the glove compartment. I shoved my Pamas in it before leaving the embassy."

Abella quickly opened the glove compartment and grabbed the pistol. Her anger had overtaken her fear and she wanted revenge. *No one will stop me from getting to America!* Abella thought as she cocked the pistol.

As the Mercedes moved forward on the right, Abella steadied herself and waited for the precise moment. She glanced in the outside door mirror and noticed the pistol extend from the sedan's passenger window. Just ahead and to the right were two large cement pillars supporting a pedestrian bridge that extended over the coastal road. Abella quickly raised the Pamas G1 and fired a single shot at the driver of the Mercedes. The driver's window exploded as the bullet impacted his skull, causing his head to burst. The black sedan violently swerved to the right, as Abella had planned, and struck the pillars exploding into a ball of fire.

"You haven't lost your skills," said Yves as he grimaced in pain. He slowed the car just before taking the off ramp to the airport. Although he was still struggling with the discomfort from his wound, the bullet had passed completely through his left shoulder.

"Abella, I won't be able to accompany you. I've got to get to the embassy's hospital. You have everything you need. Just remember, be firm and be French. There is still work to get you to America."

Yves pulled the car into the parking area of the airport, disregarded the do not enter warning signs. He stopped just outside the entry doors. Security guards standing at the entry of the terminal immediately noticed Yves's Peugeot illegally stopped. They cautiously approached the car with their automatic weapons at the ready. Abella quickly grabbed her bag from the backseat, kissed Yves on the cheek, and slowly opened the door. She was wearing tight Levis, heels, and a waist length red V-neck sweater. The guards stopped as she confidently walked toward them. As Abella approached they parted, ogling her.

19

Colleen stepped from the taxi and looked at the old colonial stable in Alexandria that she had heard so much about. She was excited, not only because she was to see the inside of Mitch's residence, but she would finally be alone with him. She quickly stepped to his door and knocked noticing that there had been recent repairs made to the old eighteenth century entrance.

"Sorry, but could you let yourself in. I've got my hands full at the moment." Mitch's muffled voice could barely be heard through the thick wooden entry.

Colleen firmly gripped the door handle with both hands and pushed with her entire body. Slowly the ancient entrance opened to reveal a hallway and Mitch juggling two wine glasses and a newly opened bottle of merlot.

"Greetings and welcome to my humble impoverished abode," Mitch said as he smiled and motioned for Colleen to enter.

Colleen laughed as she noticed a little wine spilling from one of the glasses onto the wooden floor and Mitch's brown loafers. "Mitch, let me help you with the wine." She quickly glided to his side taking the bottle and noticing the fragrance of his musk cologne.

"Your apartment really isn't that bad. The way you described it I thought I would be standing in a dilapidated colonial museum. Actually, it's rather quaint and rustic in a unique way."

"Colleen, stop with the compliments. I know it's a borderline dump, but it was the only thing available at the time. Please sit and have a little wine before we depart for the restaurant. Hope you don't mind, but the Nautical House isn't too far so I thought we could walk. Don't want to arrive too early because I suspect Jake's gotta have a cigar before our rendezvous at eight. So, in the meantime, why don't I give you a two-minute historical tour of my apartment. Keep in mind, I just moved back after I had that surprise encounter with those two uninvited guests a few weeks ago. Had to redecorate and buy a few pieces of furniture. Also, there was a repair needed on the floor and front door. But being back in the stable beats the hell out of sleeping on Sean's hard couch and having to share his bathroom. In fact, if we depart a little early, we can drop into Murph's and say hello to Sean. He's working the bar tonight."

They sat together on the sofa and Mitch began to tell her the history of the stable and Major Richard Phillips.

"Mitch, are you saying an American Revolutionary War officer died in this stable? A few years ago, I took the Alexandria ghost tour and remember the guide mentioning something about a ghost that still lurks around this area of Christ Church. I thought it was a bunch of BS. But now I'm getting chills just thinking about the fact that he died near where I'm sitting. Yuck! Maybe we should leave early for the restaurant. Call me crazy, but I'm getting the feeling he's here with us right now." Colleen moved closer to Mitch and carefully studied the room.

"Hmm . . . I'm thinking I won't comment on that last statement of yours. Just kick back, relax, and drink the wine. I'm sure the ghost is nowhere to be found." Mitch winked and smiled.

"So, this is where all the action occurred when those terrorists tried to kill you. From what I read in the newspaper, one of them died from a gunshot wound and the other went to the hospital with head trauma. Is he still alive? Colleen asked.

"Actually, they're both dead. The one that was clubbed died in the hospital the next day."

"I probably shouldn't ask this next question but being a reporter, I will anyway. I thought you told me that you were restricted from having particular items when you returned to the States. Wouldn't that restriction include a gun? Especially in the DC area. But from the reports I read, you shot one of the terrorists. How did that happen?"

"It's a long, strange story. But remember what I said about Major Phillips. He supplied the pistol that I used."

"Say what?" Colleen almost dropped her glass of wine. "How the hell can a ghost supply a gun? And how did he do it precisely at the time you needed it?"

"Colleen, I said it was strange." Mitch responded then drained his glass of wine. He stood and walked to a large heavy coat hanging from a peg behind the door. He reached into the inner breast pocket and withdrew Major Phillips flintlock pistol. Mitch slowly walked back to the couch and handed it to Colleen. "Take a close look at that ancient weapon. It saved my life."

"What the . . . where . . . how?" You're not bullshitting me, are you?"

"Nope. It was hidden under the floor. I found it in a brass chest just as the first terrorist got through the door and attacked me."

"Wait a minute! So, you're saying that Major Phillips hid this pistol in a brass chest under the floor. How did you know it was there?"

"Colleen, I said it was a very strange story. Perhaps if we leave now, I can get Sean to tell you all about Major Phillips and his hidden brass chest. He can tell the story much better than me. Besides, he has a great Irish accent, and it makes anything sound fantastic."

Mitch took the pistol from Colleen's hand and replaced it in the coat pocket. Colleen was still awestruck by what she had just heard.

"Yes, let's get going. I've gotta hear this story from your buddy, Sean. This could really make for a great editorial piece, if you don't mind."

"I thought you came empty handed without a notebook and pen," Mitch said.

"I did, but I'm sure you have a few spare pens and some paper around your apartment."

"Hmm . . . actually I'm not too sure I do." Mitch got up and looked near the fireplace.

There was a small wooden container that he routinely threw spare change. He smiled and reached into the rectangular box withdrawing a pen. "I'll give this pen to you as a gift. But you can't have it until we get to Murph's and you're taking notes on a napkin. Actually, it's the pen that the president signed the letters that ended the hearings and gave me back my life."

"I can't take that pen from you." Colleen insisted. "That's a treasure from the White House, and its sentimental value is priceless." Colleen said while shaking her head.

"No Colleen, I want you to have it. As I said before, you helped me in so many ways during those hearings. Giving you this pen is the least I can do. But you can't write a word until we're with Sean. In fact, I'll hold onto the pen until then."

Colleen slowly stood and looked longingly into Mitch's eyes. She took his hand and then kissed him on the lips. "Thank you. I'll always treasure the pen. Not because it was used by the president, but because you gave it to me."

Mitch slipped the pen into his trousers pocket and felt guilty. "There are so many things you don't know about me. Someday I'll tell you, but for now let's visit Sean." Mitch gently placed his hand on Colleen's back, and they walked out of his apartment into the cool evening air.

20

An old white Toyota sedan pulled up along the street and stopped near the Alexandria Market Square on King Street. It was seven twenty in the evening and the setting sun painted a brilliant reddish hue on the fading sky.

"We will stay here and observe those walking along the streets of Alexandria. I am sure that Ross will not take a taxi to the Nautical House restaurant. I've been told that those who reside in Alexandria enjoy walking during this time of year," Seth Hunt said while casually observing a couple walking hand in hand along the grass of the square.

"Master, forgive me for asking, but earlier today you mentioned that Colonel Ross resides near the Christ Church. We are many blocks from that location, and we cannot observe his activities from here. And how is it that you know that he is going to the Nautical House along the Potomac River?" Rahba cringed in anticipation of being struck by Hunt.

Hunt was sitting in the front passenger seat of the sedan. He didn't look at Rahba, but only shook his head. Then he slowly turned and stared causing Rahba to wince and tremble.

"You are an imbecile, and I should thrash you for questioning me! Our leader of the al-Qaeda, Osama bin Laden, has informants that tell me all. They exist in every region of Washington DC, but also throughout the United States. Do you think that I'm that ignorant to not have eyes and ears in all the establishments? I was informed minutes after Colonel Ross made reservations at the Nautical House.

"There will be two besides the Colonel dining tonight at eight. He has requested a table that looks over the Potomac River. I'm sure that he will be accompanied by the female *Washington Post* reporter who was dropped off at his residence earlier this evening. I have strategically selected this area of Alexandria because I can look along King Street and see the entrance of Murph's Irish Pub. I have been told he frequents that establishment often. I also know that most residents of Alexandria, when walking to the Nautical House, will either take King or Cameron Street. Look over my shoulder, idiot, and the street on the other side of Market Square is Cameron. Finally, there are members of the Alexandria Police Department that provide me with information.

"The police currently have a twenty-four seven stakeout observing Colonel Ross's apartment. This was established after the failed attempt to kill him. Infidels are so stupid. I would never attempt to make that same mistake again! Therefore, we are here and not near Christ Church. We will kill Ross as he walks to the restaurant tonight. We must eliminate him! He is the Satan that blocks my true purpose for being here in America. So shut up and sit. I do not want to hear any more of your ridiculous questions."

21

"Mitch, it's so beautiful this evening. Would you be disappointed if I asked that we visit with Sean another day? I just want to stroll with you along the old cobblestone streets and take a leisurely route to the Nautical House. I rarely get a chance to relax and enjoy a sunset with someone who makes me feel so content." Colleen moved closer to Mitch and entwined her arm with his.

"Sure, that's fine. In fact, let's take Cameron Street. It's a nice walk and leads straight to the restaurant. I'll point out a few old historical buildings along the way." Mitch responded.

"Great! So, I have my own personal tour guide." Colleen smiled feeling secure and warm.

They walked across Columbus Street into the cemetery of Christ Church. "I'm sure you heard the history of the church during the ghost tour many years ago, but there is a unique item that I would like to point out to you." Mitch turned and pointed at an old headstone near the brick fence encircling the church.

The brilliance of the sun had long since faded and Colleen was having difficulty reading what had been carved on the stone. She squatted and stared at the ancient slab.

"Mitch, this is over two hundred years old!" She moved closer for a better look and then gasped. "Oh my God, it's the grave of Major Richard Phillips! It says he died May 1780 and was an officer in the

1st Virginia Regiment." Colleen sprang to her feet and almost tackled Mitch as she wrapped both arms around him and buried her face in his chest. "Let's get outta here! This neighborhood creeps me out. Your ghost stories are becoming too much of a reality."

Mitch laughed and wrapped his arm around her as they walked out of the grounds of the church and onto Cameron Street. "Okay, you can relax now. Our next stop on the tour will be

Gadsby's Tavern. No spooky stories there. But it has been written that George Washington would seriously get down to some bodacious dancing and drinking in this watering hole." Mitch laughed again as Colleen glanced at him with a skeptical look.

As they approached the tavern, Mitch checked his watch. They had fifteen minutes before their scheduled rendezvous with Jake at the restaurant. Colleen was still tightly holding Mitch's arm as they moved under a light adjacent to the front of the tavern along North Royal Street. Oddly, the streets seemed to be deserted. As they read a historical brass plaque outside the main door, Mitch didn't notice the man slowly approaching in the darkness from Market Square.

"Excuse me for interrupting, Colonel Ross, but I believe we have some unfinished business to take care of."

Mitch and Coleen immediately turned and saw the gray silhouette of a man standing in the darkened shadows away from any streetlights. As Mitch strained to make out details, he noticed a gun hanging from the stranger's right hand. Colleen squeezed Mitch's arm and pulled him closer. He could feel her body trembling and hear her nervous breathing.

"What do you want from us, and how do you know my name? If it's money that you're looking for I'll throw you my wallet!" Mitch yelled, attempting to attract attention from anyone that might be nearby.

The stranger laughed loudly while taking a few steps closer to the street. "It's always about the money, isn't it? You infidel scum continuously dream of the Almighty dollar. That's what sickens me of your way of life."

Mitch noticed the man limp and realized who it was. "You son of a bitch! It's you, Seth Hunt. So, you've personally come to kill me because your puppets couldn't do it! Fine, but let the lady go. She has nothing to do with you."

Hunt seethed, raising his pistol pointing at Mitch and Colleen while slowly limping toward them. "There will be a great celebration among my followers once I have eliminated you. It will fulfill a personal jihad and avenge all those magnificent warriors you killed in the Casbah. But most importantly, it will clear my path and allow me to take the final steps in striking back at this satanic land you call America!"

Mitch whispered to Colleen, "Run as fast as you can and don't look back."

"I have waited too long for this moment. Each day I limp is a reminder of the final shot that Warrant Officer McQueen took while you ran from my residence in the Casbah. It is good that he is dead and now you will follow him to hell!"

"Go to hell, you bastard," Mitch goaded, trying to get Hunt's rage focused solely on him.

Coleen gripped Mitch's waist and looked up at him with tears streaming. "I won't leave you."

"NO . . . GO . . . NOW," Mitch yelled. But Colleen clinged even more tightly, wrapping her body around his, lurching in front of Mitch just as Hunt fired.

Seeing blood on Mitch's chest, Hunt quickly turned and hobbled toward a Toyota sedan parked down the street on Market Square. Mitch felt the red dampness on his shirt and stood in shock, thinking he had been shot. Instead, Colleen collapsed, grasping at Mitch's shirt collar and pulling him toward her. It was her blood.

"Oh Mitch," Colleen whispered. "I've fallen in love with you."

Blood oozed from the side of her chest as she gasped for air and then closed her eyes as life escaped.

Boiling with rage, Mitch gently lowered Colleen's head to the pavement and sprinted toward the murderer. While running he reached into his trousers pocket and withdrew the president's pen. Mitch raised it above his head and lunged at the limping killer driving it deep into the left shoulder and neck. Hunt screamed in agony while grasping at the pen and dropping his gun. Still struggling, he hobbled and swayed attempting to get to the car.

Rabah, running from the sedan and hidden in the darkness, slammed into Mitch, knocking him down and then kicking him in the stomach. The front car door was open, and he shoved Hunt into the passenger seat and then quickly sped off. Mitch rose from the pavement gasping for air, stunned.

22

Jake was standing near a pier in Alexandria along the Potomac River, taking his last few enjoyable draws of a fine Cuban Cohiba. In the distance he could hear soft jazz of a street musician playing a saxophone. The cool evening was perfect, and Jake was looking forward to a relaxing dinner with Mitch and Colleen. He turned toward the Nautical House and began walking up the steps to the front door when he saw a police cruiser rapidly turning onto Cameron Street with its siren blaring and lights illuminated. Jake pulled a piece of paper from his shirt pocket and read Mitch's address. *Holy shit, that police car turned in the direction of Mitch's residence. I gotta check it out!*

Jake snuffed what remained of his cigar, rapidly heading toward the sound of sirens and flashing lights. Jake had a foreboding feeling that the evening was not to be as he had hoped.

As Jake approached North Royal Street he could see a crowd had gathered near Gadsby's Tavern. The police were keeping them away from Mitch as he sat on the sidewalk and cradled the lifeless body of Colleen.

An Alexander police sergeant rested his hand on Mitch's shoulder and quietly said, "Sir, you'll have to allow the medical technicians and coroner examine the body. Plus, I've got a few questions to ask you."

Mitch wiped his tears, softly caressed Colleen's face for the last time. As he slowly stood with his bloodstained hands and clothing, he heard a familiar voice.

"Colonel, its Jake!"

Mitch's head snapped in the direction of the voice, and he immediately began walking toward the crowd as Jake maneuvered his way through the police barrier and under the tape. Mitch reached out to him. Jake's large arm wrapped around Mitch's shoulders as he consoled his old friend.

"I knew somethin' was up. Oh Lord, why did it have to be that fine young lady? Who would have done such an evil act to that precious angel?"

Mitch whispered, "It was him, it was that bastard Hunt. He was out to kill me. Colleen took the bullet that was intended for me. She jumped in front of the gun just as he fired. She saved my life and I'll never be able to thank her."

"Colonel, it was once said by a great man that every step toward the goal of justice requires sacrifice, sufferin', and struggle. We'll get that bastard, and once we do, he'll no longer have the privilege of breathin' the good Lord's air. That's how you'll be able to thank Ms. Colleen. God bless her sweet soul."

The police sergeant interrupted and apologized. "Sorry sir, but we have to ask you some questions."

Jake whispered, "Say nothin' to the police, Colonel, about knowin' Hunt. In fact, I believe that you have no clue who the killer is. I'll be waitin' over yonder once yah finish up." Jake squeezed Mitch's shoulder then walked over to a streetlamp, pulled a cigar from his shirt pocket and slowly lit the blunt end.

23

Abella firmly held her bag while attempting to quickly make her way to the Air Emirates passenger service counter in the Houari Boumediene Airport. Although many people were staring at her beauty, she avoided eye contact as she worked her way around the crowded terminal. But Abella was becoming frustrated as her every move seemed to be blocked by businessmen, families, children, stacks of luggage, and security guards.

As Abella neared the Air Emirates service counter she glanced slightly to her right and noticed a long line of passengers waiting to check in.

Damn it, now I really feel like a sitting duck standing in this line. I'm sure I was being watched by GSPC members that masquerade as ticket agents, security guards, and vendors. Abella nervously approached the end of the line. She opened her small bag and withdrew her French passport.

"*Excusez-moi mademoiselle, vous êtes Français?*"

The voice startled Abella. She froze and then reluctantly turned to see who had asked if she was French.

A tall thin Algerian gendarme was wearing a green paramilitary uniform with trousers tucked into highly polished boots and a large pistol attached to a black leather belt. Abella apprehensively raised her passport so he could see that it was French. "*Oui je suis Français.*"

The gendarme reached out and took the passport and glanced at her photo. Looking back at her he smiled showing partially decayed teeth. He thumbed through the pages noticing that there were no visas or country markings of entry or exits. He stared again at her, but this time without smiling. *"Mademoiselle, veuillez me suivre."*

Shit, he wants me to follow him! Abella thought as she grabbed her bag and attempted to keep up with the long strides of the security guard.

The gendarme headed away from the lines of passengers and service counters as he entered a darkened hallway that had two doors on either side. He opened one of the doors and threw her passport on a table near a chair within the small room.

"Qu'est-ce que vous voulez?" Abella demanded to know what the gendarme wanted. *"Nous devons parler."* The gendarme casually looked at Abella telling her that they must talk.

"J'ai rien fait de mal!" Abella sternly responded that she had done nothing wrong.

"Ta gueule!" He commanded that she shut up as he pushed her into the small room and slammed the door shut.

The gendarme made her face the table, removed his gun belt, loosened his trousers and shoved himself against her. The force caused Abella to drop her bag and reach out to break the impact. As he pressed against her, he reached around her, unbuttoning her Levis, pulling them down to her knees.

Pinned against the table, Abella did the only thing she could. She screamed hoping someone would hear as she continued to resist, but no one was nearby.

"Veuillez arrêter!" Abella pleaded to the gendarme to stop. She felt ill smelling his vial breath near her face as he bent her over the table. He stroked her nakedness as she retched and struggled to maintain consciousness.

"Ta gueule! I will speak the infidels' English to you, so I won't defile my native tongue. I have been instructed by the GSPC leadership to

kill you. But before that happens, I want to take my pleasure and defile your body as I slowly strangle you. We have waited a long time for you to leave the protection of the Catholic Basilica. Your death will be partial payment for those you killed in the Casbah. But it will also announce to that scum infidel, Ross, that your soul will be waiting for him in the pits of hell. *Allahu Akbar!*"

Just as the terrorist was repositioning himself to enter Abella, the door of the room violently slammed open and two men leaped upon the man. They threw him on the floor and began to beat him.

Abella quickly moved to the back of the room away from the fighting. She immediately pulled up her clothing and reached for the terrorist's leather gun belt on the floor beside the table. She rapidly removed the pistol and pointed it at the men.

"Arrêt!" Abella yelled for the men to stop. All three immediately froze once they noticed the gun. One of the men that had been beating the terrorist spoke as he got to his feet.

"Ma'am, its Gunny Sergeant Kotarski from the US Embassy. You're Colonel Ross's friend. That's Corporal Rodriguez sitting on top of that sorry excuse for a human being."

"Oh thank God! How did you get here? How did you know I was in this room being attacked?"

"We were having coffee at the airport café waiting for our flight to London. Corporal Rodriguez had just commented on how relaxing it was wearing casual clothes and not uniforms. I was just about ready to respond to him when I noticed you with the gendarme. You looked stressed and frightened. We saw you and that guy disappear down the hallway and figured something was up. Corporal Rodriguez mentioned that the gendarme looked a lot like one of the picture postings of dangerous GSPC terrorists that we have in our office at the embassy. Once I heard that, I didn't hesitate and headed straight to the hallway. We heard you yell."

Abella reached out and hugged the gunny, thanking him and the corporal for saving her. "Ma'am, I'm just happy that we were at the right place at the right time. But I'm sure you need to get back to the service counter. Leave the gun with me ma'am and I'll have Corporal Rodriguez escort you back to Air Emirates. I still have some unfinished business to take care of in this room."

24

The Air Emirates flight attendant smiled at the passengers and announced, *"Bienvenue à Paris. L'heure locale est trois heures vingt."*

Abella felt utterly exhausted but thankful she had finally arrived at Charles de Gaulle Airport. She glanced at her watch and confirmed that it was just as the flight attendant had announced, 3:20 p.m. She grabbed her bag and headed for the airport train station hoping to catch an express to the city and a connector to the Palais de Chaillot. What surprised Abella was that once she left the train at Passy Station, Yves's apartment was only a few minutes' walk. She also noticed, adjacent to the apartment, a small quaint brick building that displayed in its window's magnificent breads, pastries, and wine.

After what I've gone through today, I owe myself a few pleasures of life, Abella thought while looking through the window into the shop. She was pleasantly overwhelmed with all the wonderful selections and aromas of French pastries and breads just from the oven. She bought a bag full of delicate patisserie, a large baguette, cube of butter, and a bottle of cabernet. Now Abella was ready to lock herself into Yves's apartment and forget about the world except for one individual, Mitch Ross.

The cipher lock combination numbers that Yves had given Abella at the Basilica worked as planned and she entered the apartment.

The musty smell and slight humidity indicated that it had not been opened for some time. But the apartment was nothing as she had anticipated. Abella dropped her clothes bag and put the food on a small round table just inside the room to her left.

She closed and locked the door and then let her curiosity overtake her fatigue. The living room walls had large uniquely framed black and white pictures of mountains from around the world. The wooden floors were covered with exquisite handmade Persian rugs of red, black, blue, and ivory. There was an array of unusual pieces of mountain climbing equipment. Among all of this was a well-worn brown leather couch and an old wooden rocking chair.

What the hell. Yves has been holding out on us. He lives in a completely different world when he gets outside of those embassy walls. Abella examined the framed photographs and read the engraved metal placards attached identifying each mountain.

She was in awe seeing Yves in the pictures climbing the Eiger Sanction, the Matterhorn, Mount Kilimanjaro, El Capitan, Mount Everest, and Mount McKinley.

Why hasn't he mentioned this life as a mountain climber? He knew that I would see all these photographs while staying at the apartment.

Across from the furniture was a large bookshelf covering the entire wall. Abella quickly noticed that most subjects were of military history or mountain climbing techniques. Then she saw a small group of classical novels. Wedged between a French edition of Hemingway's *A Farewell to Arms* and Tolstoy's *War and Peace* was a book entitled, *Vincent Van Gogh*. She pulled the book from the shelf and opened the cover. Just as Yves had promised there was an envelope full of Euros and a note.

Abella took the note and then placed the book, which still contained the Euros, back on the shelf. Her mind was spinning with questions about Yves as she felt the soft veil of sleep overtake her.

A sparkling brilliant light pierced the living room window followed by the muted sound of a ship's horn. Although Abella wanted to roll over and continue sleeping her subconscious curiosity screamed for her to wake. Her eyes slowly opened while her mind was momentarily lost in these strange surroundings.

Abella sluggishly sat up and noticed the unusual light coming from the window. She stood and looked out discovering a wide river flowing near the apartment. There were large, long boats with many people sitting and gazing out on the top decks. Then Abella looked toward the brilliant sparkling glow that was lighting up the evening sky. She was shocked at its beauty and wanted to find a better view.

Running through a bedroom of the apartment Abella noticed a door leading to a small terrace. She quickly stepped out feeling the fresh evening air and took in the beauty of the mysterious illuminated flashing lights. Then she realized that not more than two city blocks away was the magnificent Eiffel Tower. It was breathtaking, as the entire structure glimmered and searchlights on top made it a beacon throughout Paris's night sky. But as soon as she had discovered it the sparkling lights dimmed and the Eiffel Tower became a shadow.

Abella was disappointed as the darkened sky once again surrounded the famous structure.

She wished it was still aglow and that she had been able to share the magical moment with Mitch. She found her bottle of cabernet and uncorked it in the kitchen. Abella noticed a nice wine glass in a cabinet above the sink and poured a healthy amount of the aged French liquid.

She returned to the couch and let her mind wander as she sipped the wine. Abella noticed more climbing equipment near an adjacent end table. As she looked closer, she realized that the gear had been piled atop a telephone. As the wine was having its warm magical effect, Abella thought of her friends that she had once known at

Georgetown University. She leaned back into the cushions and rested the glass on the crowded end table. As her mind continued to wander a piece of the gear fell from the table and startled Abella.

I wish I could call Mitch, but I have no clue where he is and I'm sure he keeps a low profile considering what he has gone through recently.

She felt the pain of loneliness and reached for her travel bag pulling out an old address book. Abella flipped through the pages and stopped at a name she had written down years ago while living in the DC area. *I wonder if Mallory still lives in that apartment in Georgetown.*

Damn, we had great parties in that small two-bedroom paradise! We were like sisters that shared everything. She was the greatest and a helluva soccer player. It's a shame I lost contact with her over the years.

Abella ran her fingers over the faded page wishing that she could go back in time and relive those wonderful moments. Then she glanced at the phone and without hesitating pushed the gear to the floor. She cradled the phone in her lap and began to dial the number of her long-lost friend. It was a six-hour difference between DC and Paris, but Abella didn't care that it was midnight in the City of Lights.

25

"Hello. Whoever is calling please speak up because this is a terrible connection."

"Is this Mallory Paulus that went to Georgetown University and played on the women's soccer team?" Abella excitedly blurted.

"Okay, I'm not interested in whatever you're trying to sell. Please take me off your damn phone list. Oh, by the way, get a better phone!" Mallory hung up.

Damn it. I know that was Mallory, Abella thought in frustration. She quickly redialed the number and waited eagerly as a hunter waits to sweeten a shot before pulling the trigger. As soon as she heard the phone being answered on the other end, Abella rapidly spoke.

"Mallory, please don't hang up! It's Abella, your soccer buddy from Georgetown. Don't hang up . . . please," she yelled into the phone.

"Who? What? The connection is bad. Did you say Abella?"

"Yes, yes it's Abella!"

"Oh my God, Abella Amari?"

"Mallory, I can't believe that you still live in Georgetown."

"Abella, it's really you! I'll be damned. I've gotta get you up to speed on my life and why I'm still living in this old apartment. Do you have time to listen?"

"Of course, Mallory, I'm all ears."

"Once I graduated from Georgetown and you went back to

Algeria, I looked for a job. With my accounting degree it didn't take long before I was working for a company in DC called Deloitte. The hours are long during tax season, but the pay is good. Unfortunately, it's not enough to allow me to upgrade into a bigger DC apartment, so I stayed put in this old two room abode. It works for me, and the rental price hasn't really increased that much over the years. Plus, I grab the metro and it takes me within two blocks of the office.

"So Abella, please tell me that you're coming out to visit your old girlfriend. I need something exciting to look forward to and break up this monotonous lifestyle of mine. I still haven't found Mister Right, and there hasn't been a wild party in this apartment since you left years ago. By the way, how is your life? I need to disengage my motor-mouth and let you talk. How are your parents doing, and are you still living in Algeria?"

Abella paused before answering to gather her thoughts. She noticed Yves's note on the carpet near the couch. Abella picked it up; it contained information on her American visa and departure from Paris to DC.

"Abella, are you still there? I hope I didn't say anything that might have disturbed you."

"I'm still here, but there is so much I must tell you. It would take all night and cost a small fortune in telephone charges. I'm currently in Paris staying at a friend's apartment. I'm hoping that within a month I'll be departing for DC. It's a one-way trip, and I'm eager to start a new life in the States."

"What! You're actually coming back to the DC area? To live? Abella, you must stay with me! It'll be like old times except we're older, wiser, and hopefully we won't drink as much.

Please let me know when you'll arrive. I'll definitely pick you up at Dulles International. Oh Abella, I've been down in the dumps for a while and there has been absolutely no excitement in my life. You've really made me feel great! If you were here right now, we would break open a bottle of champagne to celebrate."

"Actually Mallory, I believe we'll need to be pounding bourbon with what I'll tell you once we're together."

"Damn . . . I can't wait. Get your ass over to this side of the Atlantic, *pronto!*" Mallory laughed

"I'll give you a call once I figure out all the flight details. You take care. Bye for now, Mallory. Talk to you soon."

"Okay, will definitely look forward to your call. Bye."

Abella waited to hear the line disconnect and then placed the phone on the end table. She took a sip of her wine and a closer look at Yves's note:

> *Dear Abella,*
>
> *By the time you read this note you should be safe and secure in my apartment. Please feel at home and don't be reluctant to use whatever you need from my meager household possessions. The reason I didn't inform you earlier of the information contained in this note was of a security concern. I suspected some of the individuals within the church were not trustworthy. I didn't want to inadvertently discuss your visa and flight plans from Paris to DC in case someone was listening. French intelligence had briefed me that the GSPC had received information from someone within the church that you were to be leaving. Additional information was revealed that the terrorist organization was planning an attack on the Basilica to capture and kill you. That is why we had to expedite your departure out of Algeria. Now that you are in Paris you must contact the US Embassy and request a meeting with James Grose. He is an American diplomat working closely with me and is well aware of your situation.*
>
> *James has arranged with the embassy consular office for you to receive a US visa. All of this will be accomplished during your meeting with him. I recommend that you contact him as soon as possible. He is waiting to hear from you. Once*

you have attained your visa, James will schedule your flight to the States. Good luck, Abella, and I hope that one day we will meet again.

   Sincerely Yves.

26

"Master, I must take you to a hospital immediately. Your wound is much more serious than what you might think," Rabah pleaded as he glanced at Seth Hunt slumped over in the front seat of the car, the pen grotesquely protruding from his neck.

Hunt moved his head slightly to the left without opening his eyes. He reeked of stale sweat and piss. Blood oozed from the wound and the excruciating pain had created an unbearable migraine. He was overcome with nausea and could barely respond to Rabah.

"No! Take me to the mosque, imbecile!" he seethed.

Rabah sped through the darkness of night as the sedan headed northwest on Leesburg Pike. As he looked in the distance, Rabah saw the hazy cloud of light above the mosque. He glanced at his watch and cursed. The final prayer of the evening had concluded, which meant vehicle congestion from people leaving the main parking lot and merging onto access roads.

Rabah drove to the rear of the mosque and enter the back door of the sanctuary. He had not noticed that Hunt had completely slumped over and was slumped in the front seat, semiconscious and no longer moving.

"Master, can you hear me. We are at the mosque, and I will get help!" Rabah quickly departed the sedan and ran to the rear entrance.

As he swung the door open, he practically ran into two large men departing.

"You must help me get my master into the mosque. He's been wounded and needs medical assistance immediately," Rabah pleaded.

The men followed Rabah to the car and removed Hunt, recoiling when they saw the bloody pen protruding from his neck.

"Your master seems to be gravely injured. Should he not go to a hospital?" one of the men commented.

"No, he will be treated in the mosque's clinic!" Rabah directed the men down a broad hallway and then entered the clinic where he recognized a former al-Qaeda medic who had fought in Iraq and Afghanistan. The man was sleeping in a chair in the corner of the large white room.

"Wakeup! There is an emergency! My master has been gravely injured and requires immediate medical assistance."

The startled medic jumped from his chair and pulled a gurney from an adjoining room. He grabbed latex gloves from a dispenser and prepared a syringe of morphine. The two men propped Hunt into a sitting position on the gurney.

"Thank you for your assistance, but now you two can leave the clinic," Rabah said.

"How did that pen become imbedded in his shoulder and neck?" the medic asked.

"It is not your position to ask questions," Rabah scolded. "This man is the leader of the Algerian GSPC and is under direct orders from Osama bin Laden. Make sure you take good care of him or there will be consequences."

The medic injected Hunt with morphine and carefully removed the patient's bloodstained shirt. He closely examined Hunt's wound and cleansed the area with a medical saline solution. Then he began to prepare for extraction of the pen and stem the bleeding. The medic carefully grasped the pen and slowly removed it. As the medic rubbed the blood from the pen he gasped.

"This is from the White House! You said not to question, but I do not want to be implicated in anything this man has done!"

"I'm sorry, but you already are! Shut up and continue."

As he stitched up the wound the medic described to Rabah his initial findings. "The patient's heart tones are normal without palpitations, and there is no damage to a major artery. But his breathing seems to be erratic, perhaps from a partially collapsed lung. I suggest an x-ray from a local hospital to determine how much damage was done."

"How many times must I tell you that my master will be taken care of here in the clinic and no other location. Now clean him up and continue to stitch the wound."

The morphine dulled the pain, and Hunt roused.

"There will be no trip to a hospital. I feel fine except for a slight breathing problem. Finish stitching my wound. There is much work and planning to do before Rabah and I depart for Chicago!" Hunt said, weakly, as he stared at the medic.

"Chicago? Why must we go to that city, Master?" Rabah blurted, immediately knowing he would be punished for asking.

Hunt slowly stood without saying a word and ignored the medic's efforts to close the wound. He took a few steps toward Rabah, taking a scalpel from an adjacent counter, raising it above his head. With his free hand grabbed Rabah's throat.

Rabah fell to his knees. "Master, please forgive me! I'm a fool for questioning you. I promise, as Allah is my witness, I will never question you again! Please spare my life!"

Hunt paused as Rabah noticed the demented glare in Hunt's eyes flicker and slowly disappear. The morphine was suppressing his rage. Hunt lowered the scalpel and released his grasp.

As Hunt sat back down on the gurney, Rabah breathed a sigh of relief and whispered a thankful prayer to Allah.

27

There was a gray overcast in the cool morning air as Paris awoke. Abella was up early anxiously waiting to call the US Embassy. She brewed a cup of coffee and sat at a small round table in Yves's kitchen, rereading the note that he had placed in the book along with the Euros.

Abella jotted down the diplomat's name, James Grose, who she was to contact at the embassy. Then she slowly wrote his office phone number making sure that there would be no dialing errors.

Oh God, I hope Mr. Grose remembers who I am and why I'm calling, Abella thought as she walked to the kitchen window looking down and noticing large barges slowly moving along the river Seine.

She glanced at a small clock near the stove and noticed that it was almost eight. Pausing, Abella hoped the man would be in his office. *I can't wait any longer.*

"US Embassy. Jim Grose speaking. May I help you?"

"Mr. Grose, this is Abella Amari. Colonel Yves Dureau told me to call you concerning a visa and flight information."

There was no immediate response, and Abella thought that perhaps the American diplomat had hung up. She waited a moment longer, her hands shaking.

"Sorry Miss Amari for the delay. I was looking for your file in a locked cabinet near my desk. Yes, Colonel Dureau is a good man and a great ally. Now, let's get to the point. Is there any chance that you can come to the embassy today and discuss the details of what needs to be accomplished? It would really move things along."

"Oh yes, I can come to the embassy today. What time would be convenient for you?" *He probably doesn't want to discuss this on the phone for security reasons,* she thought.

"Can you be at the security entry point at ten? My schedule is open until one."

"Yes, I will be there at ten."

"Great, see you then."

Abella hung up and ran to the bedroom. Grabbing the French doors that led to the terrace, she flung them open. Standing outside she felt the cool breeze blow through her hair and the thin loosely tied robe that she wore. She gazed across the river at the Eifel Tower, then closed her eyes and took a deep breath. Abella realized this was to be the next chapter of her life.

28

Mitch looked across the partially frozen waters where the Potomac and Anacostia merged. In the distance, he could see the Washington Monument. The chill of the morning seeped through his uniform. He was still extremely fatigued and emotionally upset by the death of Colleen. He couldn't free his mind of the constant guilt he felt. *Why did she have to take the bullet that was intended for me? She was so innocent and naive to all the darkness and hate in this world.*

Mitch pulled the woolen scarf tighter around his neck and fastened the top button of his heavy military coat. He took a deep breath and then entered the Defense Intelligence Agency headquarters at Bolling Air Force Base. The ominously large rectangular building seemed to be as much glass as it was metal.

"Sir, please proceed to your right, remove your coat, and enter the detector," an armed military security guard instructed Mitch upon entering the DIA facility.

Once through the metal detector, he affixed a special DIA badge to one of his shirt epaulets and retrieved his coat.

"Can you tell me where the office of the director is located?"

"Yes sir. Take those stairs just to the right of where you're standing. Once at the top make an immediate left. The fourth office on the right is the director's. You can't miss it."

Mitch had five minutes before his scheduled meeting with DIA Director Admiral Scott, who had requested the meeting. Mitch feared the encounter would not be pleasant. He expected to be dressed down by the admiral. Mitch had heard that many at the agency thought that he had been a loose cannon in Algeria.

Mitch noticed the oversized metal plaque that designated the director's office. He firmly grasped the large decorative handle and opened the door. Sitting off to the left behind a rose-colored wooden desk was the admiral's receptionist.

"May I help you?"

"Yes ma'am. I'm Colonel Mitch Ross and I have a meeting with Director Admiral Scott at his request."

"Yes, I see you on his calendar. Have a seat and he should be available shortly. Within a moment the receptionist returned to her desk.

"You may see the director now."

Mitch placed his military coat and hat on a couch adjacent to the receptionist and entered the huge office, its walls adorned with large paintings of naval ships in combat, military memorabilia on tabletops, and a bulky desk near the back wall where the admiral sat.

"Colonel, take the seat over here near my desk."

The admiral repositioned some documents on his desk and leaned back in his brown leather chair. He reached out and grabbed his coffee cup, taking a mouthful.

"Colonel, I just finished reading your military record. Specifically what you've accomplished, or attempted to accomplish, in the past couple years. Seems as though things began to go downhill for you when you were stabbed by that terrorist during a diplomatic reception in Algiers. Followed by a close call while riding in an embassy vehicle. Then surviving the attack on the US Embassy by the GSPC. The after-action report stated that you were in your residence when they attacked and fought your way out before your house was destroyed. You and a companion took out several of the terrorists and saved the lives of State Department and Marine personnel during the fighting within the embassy. But it was the attempt to rescue the POW, Captain Seth Hunt, that concerns me. You went well beyond the charter of a Defense Department attaché's mission. That, at a minimum, could result in a reprimand or an Article 15. Worst case, going to prison and losing everything that you've worked for in your military career. I am aware that the president recommended that Senator Levin end the congressional investigation.

"It's been noted that you experienced what appeared to be psychological medical issues during cross examination. In fact, during this past year, you've been seen by several physicians because of the stabbing incident, numerous blows to the head, and a gunshot wound to the shoulder. As the director of the DIA, I have never read of any attaché experiencing what you have gone through. How are you feeling now colonel?"

"Physically I'm fine, admiral."

"Perhaps you are, but mentally I suspect that you're far from stable."

"Sir, I feel fine."

"I've got news for you Colonel Ross. Being a member of the DIA, you must not only be physically fit, but more importantly, you must be of sound mind! What you have experienced would mentally challenge the strongest individual. I'm ordering you to take some time away from your military duties. You need to get away and clear your mind. Do you understand, colonel?"

Mitch squirmed. "Yes sir."

"You'll take sixty days, and I'll personally sign your leave paperwork in case there are any questions concerning the length of time off. During that time, you will also go to Walter Reed for psychiatric evaluations and treatment if warranted. I want to make sure there you are sound when, and if, you come back to work. My receptionist will complete the documents prior to your departure today. Do you have any questions?"

"No sir."

"Good! You take care, colonel. Tell my receptionist to come into my office. Remember, you will not leave this building without proper papers establishing two months away from any work beginning tomorrow. After that period of time, you will directly report back to me."

Mitch stood and saluted the admiral, reluctantly responding, "Thank you, sir." Then he turned toward the door.

"Oh, by the way," The admiral said just before Mitch departed. "There'll be no disciplinary charges levied against you. What you have experienced has been hell. I want you to kick back and relax. You've earned it!"

Mitch entered the outer office and informed the receptionist that the admiral wanted to see her. As he waited for her return his mind began to wander. *What the hell am I going to do with all that free time? If I truly had 60 days off, I would get on a jet to Algiers and find Abella. But I can't because of those damn shrink appointments at Walter Reed!*

29

The taxi pulled up outside of Yves's apartment. Abella had been anxiously waiting and quickly jumped into the back seat.

"*S'il vous plait,* 2 Avenue Gabriel," she said.

The driver responded, *"Oui, l'ambassade américaine. Très intéressant!"*

Abella thought that his statement was quite odd. So, she asked why. *"Pourquoi c'est intéressant?"*

As the taxi driver departed for the embassy he responded, *"Parce que vous êtes jeune et joli. L'Amérique sera bonne pour vous."*

Abella blushed and thought, *yes America will be good for me if I can find Mitch and he still wants me.*

She responded, *"Merci, monsieur."*

The cab passed the gardens of the Champs Elysees and pulled to the curb just outside a majestic four-story, neoclassical building. Abella peered through the taxi's window and could see the American flag extending out from a second-floor balcony. A metal plaque near the security checkpoint adjacent to the Place de la Concorde read, Embassy of the United States.

"Merci beaucoup." Abella said to the driver as she paid the fare and headed toward the security guard standing outside of the checkpoint entrance.

"Bonjour, puis-je vous aider?" the guard said with a heavy American accent.

Abella didn't hesitate and responded in perfect American English while showing her French passport. "I hope you can help me. I have an appointment with James Grose at ten this morning."

The guard motioned for Abella to enter the security building. Where she was asked to submit her passport for examination. After reviewing her document and the embassy visitor access list, a phone call was made to the main embassy compound and Abella could see a balding middle-aged man approaching. As he entered, he turned and smiled while reaching out to shake her hand.

"Hello. I'm Jim Grose, and you must be Abella. So glad to finally meet you. Yves had said so many nice things about you, including your ability to speak American English like a native."

"It's so good to meet you Mr. Grose, but to be honest, I really need to brush up on my American speaking skills."

"Well, let's go to my office and work on that. Oh, by the way, I haven't had coffee this morning. Would you like a cup?" Jim Grose asked.

The guard returned her passport and they left the security building walking toward the large embassy entrance.

"That sounds great, thank you." Abella said as she felt her nerves begin to settle.

As they entered the embassy she immediately noticed the beautiful décor and extravagant entry room. Jim motioned toward the elevators and Abella observed that he hit the third-floor button. *Obviously, this lavish embassy is one of America's crème de la crème,* Abella thought while the elevator doors closed. As they reached the third floor, she could smell freshly brewed coffee and saw a small café that had pastries, juice, and hot beverages.

"This is our little third-floor snack bar just outside my office. It makes great coffee and French pastries. Would you like something to eat?" Jim asked.

"Just coffee, black, thanks." Abella responded.

Besides a few metal filing cabinets and a desk covered with papers and a computer, there was no interior decorating. The walls were stark white, and the only colorful item in the room was a calendar hanging on the wall. But what made his office beautiful was a window that looked out over the embassy gardens and in the distance was the Champs Elysees.

Jim motioned for Abella to take a seat near his desk as he unlocked one of the cabinets and withdrew a large bulky file. Setting it carefully near where she was sitting, he slowly opened her file. Abella noticed official correspondence from the French Embassy in Algiers. Then she saw something that made her heart race—a picture of her and Mitch when they attended the Bastille Day reception in Algiers. Abella reached out and touched the picture as her eyes began to tear. Jim noticed that she was getting emotional.

"That is such a lovely photograph of you and Colonel Ross. I can tell that you miss him greatly. Perhaps I can help you." Jim moved a few of the items within the file and then withdrew a United Airlines packet. He pulled a ticket from the envelope and handed it to Abella. As she reached out, he noticed her hand shaking.

"I'm sorry Mr. Grose, but it's been so long since I've seen Mitch. That picture brought back so many memories."

"I understand. You two look so happy in the photo. I'm hoping that this airline ticket will help you find the colonel. By the way, if you notice it's a one-way ticket to Washington Dulles International. That means I'll need to borrow your passport for a few moments and run down to the consular office. Getting your US visa has already been worked out. The only remaining issue is the actual visa being stamped in your passport. I apologize for leaving you here alone."

Before Abella could respond Jim took her passport and departed. She reached across the desk and removed the picture from the file. Abella stood and walked to the window.

Looking out at the garden below she thought of Mitch and walking with him through the roses at the US Embassy in Algiers. She glanced again at the photo and softly began to cry.

— • —

"I'm so sorry, Abella, that I was away much longer than I had intended to be. It wasn't because of the visa, but I saw the Chief of Station Tom Lopez, and we discussed the heightened terrorist threat here in Paris." He sat at his desk.

"I apologize if what I'm about to say alarms you, but it is important that you are aware of the situation. Tom recommended that we get you out of France as soon as possible. Communications intercepted from Algiers indicate that GSPC operatives here in Paris have been directed to kill you. They are aware you are someplace in the city, so it is imperative that we get you on a flight to DC now. I have changed your reservations, and you will be departing this evening. I'm sorry, but for your safety you must immediately gather your belongings. Contact no one from this point on until you are in the States."

Abella nodded. As if the news were expected.

"I have arranged for an embassy driver and security agent to take you back to where you're staying in Paris. Pack and return to the embassy ASAP. The driver and agent will wait for you. I can only guarantee your safety if you're within the security of this embassy. Once you return, I will accompany you to Charles de Gaulle International."

Since her departure from the protection of the Catholic Basilica, Abella had been in the crosshairs of the GSPC. She also felt bad about not being able to contact her old friend from Georgetown, Mallory. Calling her now with the updated departure plans would be too risky.

30

Seth Hunt had ordered Rabah to stop only when they needed fuel. He did so, speeding in the Toyota from Washington toward Chicago at eighty miles per hour. Hunt had slept much of the way, finally speaking as they sped along I-70 by Indianapolis.

"I have called a meeting early tomorrow morning with warriors of al-Qaeda. It will be north of Chicago at a location you don't need to know... and may never know." Hunt began laughing like a madman.

Rabah continued to drive without responding, but his thoughts churned with fear. North of the city? A meeting with warriors of al-Qaeda? What is the purpose of this meeting? Are there many al-Qaeda living near the great city of Chicago? *Please Allah, don't let me be a part of this? Help me to find a way to escape.*

As the sun cast a slim reddish color along the horizon of Lake Michigan, Hunt could see the impressive skyline of Chicago in the distance.

"Our timing is excellent. Continue through the city heading north. There is no reason for us to stop and sightsee, I am on a mission that only Allah and Osama bin Laden know of the details. From this point on you will listen very closely to my directions. If you make an error and we lose time, I will punish you in such a way that your family will never recognize you! That is if you live through the beatings." Hunt hysterically laughed as he repositioned himself in the front seat of the car to get a better view of the city.

31

Abella sat nervously waiting for her flight at Charles de Gaulle International. She bought a magazine but was merely turning the pages. It wasn't a feeling of excitement while waiting, but one of foreboding. Although she had told herself not to scrutinize the other passengers, her paranoia overwhelmed any logical thoughts she might have had. Anyone resembling a North African was automatically suspect to be a potential GSPC assassin. Unfortunately for Abella, there seemed to be a lot of North Africans on her flight.

Finally, the announcement to board was made and Abella anxiously entered the large airbus. She was thankful that her seat was adjacent to a window, hoping to catch up on sleep during the long flight. But she also knew sleep might be impossible depending on who sat beside her.

As the plane began to fill, she glared at each boarding passenger. A slender dark-haired man with a full beard approached, checking seat numbers. He placed his bag in the overhead compartment, stared at Abella, and then broadly smiled. She immediately felt ill, quickly turning away, and tried to control the shaking of her body. She felt trapped. The man took the seat next to her and she could smell his foul breath.

Abella frantically tried to think of possible options depending on what he might do.

"Excuse me, but I believe you're sitting in my seat," a young woman said softly to the man beside Abella.

"That is impossible, I don't make idiotic mistakes like that. Continue down the aisle. I'm sure your seat is near the toilets," the man said, flipping his left hand arrogantly as if to tell her to move on.

"I'm sorry sir, but my ticket indicates seat 63J. Perhaps yours is 63H," the young woman insisted as she held her ticket so others could see it.

"I don't care what your ticket indicates, this is my seat!" the man huffed loudly enough for a flight attendant to hear.

"Is there a problem? Young lady, you're holding up others that would like to take their seats. Can I see your ticket, please?" the United Airline flight attendant politely asked.

In the meantime, the slender man sat back down and turned toward Abella. The man smiled at Abella and arrogantly whispered, *"Elle est un cochon américain!"*

Loudly and defiantly, Abella stated in perfect English so others could hear, "That is disgusting what you just said to me! That young woman is not an American pig! If there is a pig among us, it's you!"

The flight attendant immediately stepped toward the slender man and demanded to see his ticket. "Sir, I would like to see your ticket, please! This young woman's ticket indicates that you are sitting in her seat, 63J."

The man angrily looked at the attendant and then at Abella. He could no longer contain his rage and grabbed Abella by the throat. As he squeezed her neck with his right hand, he pushed the attendant away with his left. The flight attendant fell backward while Abella gagged and struggled to free herself. She could feel his fingernails digging and tearing deep into the sides of her neck.

"No one calls me a pig without being punished, especially a woman!" the bearded man yelled in French as his hand tightened around Abella's throat.

Abella continued her fight to pull free from the madman's death grip, as the flight attendant screamed for the air marshal.

Nearby passengers seemed to be stunned and did nothing until a middle-aged woman sitting in the row behind Abella lifted her laptop computer and angrily whispered, "Shit, all I wanted was a quiet peaceful flight back to DC." She then slammed her laptop against the man's head with such force his arms dropped to his side and his face fell forward against the seat in front of him.

Abella immediately pushed him down between the seats and the young woman sat on his back.

As the air marshal approached. "Well ladies, it appears you have the situation well in hand. With passengers like you, I'll be unemployed!"

The young woman stood as the air marshal leaned over and handcuffed the bearded man before taking him off the jet. The madman glared at Abella while being pulled away and whispered in French, *"On va te tuer, cochon."*

The man was an assassin. His parting words spoke of her impending death.

"Are you okay?" the young woman asked Abella as she sat next to her.

"I am now. Thank God that creep is off this jet."

"I'll drink to that!" the woman sitting behind Abella said as she examined her computer. "I should of wacked that bastard a few more times."

Abella noticed the flight attendant standing nearby helping people with their carry-on baggage. "Excuse me, but when the beverages are served, I would like to buy a round of wine or maybe something a little stronger for these two ladies that helped me."

The attendant turned and leaned toward Abella. "With what you just went through, United Airlines will be more than happy to buy the first round. Believe me, if I could join the three of you I would, but my drink would be served in a shot glass."

Abella smiled and thanked the flight attendant, then turned to the young woman and said, "I'm sorry it's taken so long to introduce myself, but I'm Abella Amari. Thank you so much for being persistent about the seat. I'm afraid to think what that crazy man might have done to me had you not distracted him."

"Actually, it was nothing. I hate it when someone is wrong and doesn't want to admit to it. He could have just moved and there wouldn't have been any issues. I don't understand why people can be so stubborn at times. Oh, by the way, my name is Laura Lewis," the young woman said as she took Abella's hand and shook it.

"Laura, I'm glad we'll be sitting next to each other on this flight. Unfortunately, I believe that man had no intention to move. He was evil. But let's not talk about him anymore. So why were you in Paris? I notice that you're wearing a James Madison University sweatshirt," Abella said as she attempted to change the subject to deflect why she was attacked.

"I was fortunate to be able to study abroad in Paris at the University of Sorbonne for a year. It was a great experience, and I met so many wonderful people. Oh, I almost forgot. I have a bag of popcorn in my backpack and two bottles of water. Would you like to help me consume this ridiculously large bag? I get nervous flying and I eat to calm my nerves. But if I eat this entire bag of popcorn, United will have to get a forklift to help me deplane at Dulles International."

Abella laughed and finally felt relieved.

32

Jake approached the door of the old stable apartment near the historical Christ Church and softly knocked. It was midmorning and the spring sun painted its rays along the old parched wooden door. It was a beautiful start to the day as tourists gathered in the colonial church yard to begin guided tours of the famous structure that had once been President Washington's house of worship.

There was no response to the knocking, but the man persisted while calling out to the occupant.

"Colonel, I know you're in thar. You've gotta open up and get on with yah life. It's not healthy," the man yelled as he continued to knock harder on the door. He struck the door with even more force.

"Please, Mitch, at least answer me. Yah have shut yourself in that small room for too long. Let me take yah out for a late breakfast and get some sunshine on yah face. You can't live yah life like this. Yes, it was tragic what happened to that young angel, Colleen. I know it's hard to turn the page when yah know someone won't be in the next chapter. But yah must turn that page of yah life. Please, Mitch, if nothin' else do it for me. Come on don't be like this."

Then from behind the door a broken voice was barely audible.

"Please, Jake, go away. I'm the reason why Colleen is dead, and the others perished in the Casbah. I also know that I'll never see Abella again and she'll forever be just a loving memory. Please leave."

"Mitch, yah wrong. Those that are no longer with us were not yah fault. And I know that Abella would neva give up lookin' for yah. No not her. She has too much love for yah residin' in her heart. Open up this door and let's talk so othas can't hear us."

"Jake, for now please just go away. I'm not ready to face that next chapter. Please just leave," Mitch responded as he sat up from where he had been sleeping on the couch. He kicked the empty bottles of bourbon that were lying near him on the floor. There was a severe pain in his head and his body hurt as he attempted to stand.

Mitch slowly hobbled to the small bathroom and turned on the light. Peering into the mirror he stared at a face that was unrecognizable. His blue eyes had sunken deep into his face and appeared black. They were surrounded by large creases that only occur from weeks of little sleep. His stubble had grown into an unkempt beard of light brown and gray.

His soiled clothes hung from his body, and he couldn't remember how many days had passed since changing them. He reeked. Mitch realized that he was no longer the man that dreamed of a wonderful future. He didn't care anymore because those dreams had melted away in disappointment and violence.

He dragged his feet while moving from the bathroom to his heavy coat hanging from a peg behind the door. He reached into an inner pocket and withdrew a 9mm Beretta. It was the gun that Seth Hunt had dropped after being stabbed by Mitch. He pulled back on the spine of the weapon that forced a bullet into the chamber. Mitch tightly grasped the gun and slipped his index finger onto the trigger, slowly raising the instrument of death to end his suffering.

Looking around the one room apartment he felt that his life had ultimately been a failure. *It has come to this final failure in my life. I have no one, I have nothing, and I reside in this shithole. There is nothing to live for.*

He pointed the pistol at his face and sat down on the couch. He stared at a blank wooden wall and began to cry. Then from behind he heard a quiet voice that startled him.

"Stop, colonel, she is here," the voice whispered.

As Mitch quickly turned, he saw the fleeting image of a ghostly profile.

"What? She is what? Don't leave now, tell me more! What do you mean?" Mitch yelled in desperation. Then he jumped to his feet as the gun fell and hit the floor skidding across to the fireplace.

As he stood defiantly with hands clenched looking up toward the tall ceiling near the front door, Mitch yelled, "It was you, Major Phillips! Again, you return, but what is it you're attempting to tell me? There's no one here other than you, but perhaps I'm just losing my mind."

As Mitch continued to stare upward where the original stable loft had been, and Major Phillips' deathbed, the ghost reappeared, pointing to a pile of dirty clothes near Mitch's heavy coat hanging behind the door.

"What the hell are you trying to tell me?" Mitch screamed. "I've not worn those sweats since leaving Algeria!"

Mitch quickly moved to the clothes and picked up the sweatpants. He glanced up once again at the ghost of Major Phillips and noticed that he was no longer pointing. The ghost was looking back at Mitch nodding its head and then disappearing.

Mitch fell to his knees shaking. He realized that he was losing his sanity and his grip on reality. *What the hell am I doing? Did I really see and hear that ghost? Why am I holding these old unwashed sweats?*

As Mitch was ready to throw the pants down, he noticed a burgundy color within the pocket of the pants. He reached into the pocket and withdrew a long silk ribbon that smelled of jasmine. It had been Abella's. He stood frozen as tears streamed. Mitch clutched the ribbon and once again collapsed on the couch.

33

The taxi pulled up along the M street curb in Georgetown, and Abella paid the driver as she grabbed her luggage. It had been years since she stood in front of Mallory's apartment complex and noticed there hadn't been many changes. She had experienced some of the greatest moments of her young college life on M street in Georgetown, frequenting its popular restaurants, bars, and high-end shops. It had always been the central part of the Georgetown experience, especially for students at the nearby university. But now she was viewing life from a different perspective.

Abella was no longer that carefree happy-go-lucky college student. A darkness had descended, and paranoia replaced her once cheerful disposition. She was cautious about everything, especially using a phone. Her mind was forever thinking that terrorists might have followed her to DC. So Abella had taken a taxi direct from Dulles International to Georgetown without notifying Mallory. She prayed Mallory would be at home the Saturday afternoon she arrived.

Abella smiled when she noticed that the apartment entry still comprised of the old buzzer intercom located three steps up from the sidewalk. She pressed the third button from the bottom and held her breath hoping for a response. Finally, a groggy sounding woman's voice was heard over the intercom.

"Okay, who the hell is buzzing my apartment? You just interrupted my beauty sleep and I'm fighting a killer hangover. It was a wild late Friday night for me, damn it!"

Abella began to laugh and pressed the response button. "Why aren't you drinking a double Bloody Mary to sober up like we did years ago after a wild Friday night?"

Mallory rushed to the door giving her old roomy a bear hug as they danced along the sidewalk.

People walking near them stopped and began to laugh as the two young women giggled and frolicked.

"What the hell, Abella? This surprise is better than a bachelorette party on a beach in Jamaica! Holy shit, why didn't you call me to pick you up at the airport?"

"Mallory, it's a long story and better said inside your apartment. So, I hope you haven't drained all the wine and liquor in your booze cabinet? By the way, do you still have that booze cabinet?"

"Hell yes I do, and we need to visit it right now in spite of my hangover!"

With that said, Abella and Mallory gathered her luggage, and they ran up the stairs to Mallory's third story apartment.

The hours passed as Abella painfully explained what had happened since her graduation from Georgetown University. She and Mallory had stretched their emotions to the limits as Abella had relived her life in words over two bottles of cabernet and crying through countless boxes of tissues.

"Oh my God, Abella, you should feel blessed that you're still alive! Your life has been so damn different than mine. I get up each morning and go to work counting the days until Friday night. You, on the other hand, spent each day helping patients in hospitals, conspiring with diplomats, or fighting terrorists. But there is one thing I can guarantee, now that you'll be living with me. The most danger that will come your way will be fighting off all the guys in the local watering holes here in Georgetown. You're still as beautiful as you were during our college days. It's going to be a blast having my soccer sidekick with me again."

Abella smiled, giving Mallory a long heartfelt hug. Then she said, "To be honest, I might look the same, but inside there are so many scars. Also, my heartaches for that colonel that I met and fell in love with in Algeria. I've got to find him, and I need you to help me. The last I heard he was testifying to a Congressional Investigation Committee on Capitol Hill. That's all I know. I don't know where he is or if he still wants me."

Abella began to softly cry as she raised her glass and sipped the last of her wine. Mallory sat back and reflected on everything she had heard.

"Excuse me? But I believe that colonel of yours was the guy giving it to all those asshole congressmen? Abella, he became as popular as a rock star here in the DC area, and maybe the entire US. I know who he is because we all talked about him at work during the hearings. He was all over the *Washington Post* and CNN news. My God, Abella, you fell in love with Colonel Mitch Ross!"

Abella dropped her wine glass.. "WHAT ARE YOU SAYING! YOU KNOW HIS NAME?"

Without answering, Mallory, pointed to a stack of newspapers piled near her garbage can in the kitchen. "My dance card is empty for the rest of the day and there are at least two months of weekend *Post* editions in the kitchen. I save them for the discount coupons, but usually end up just throwing the stack away when it gets too high. Let's get to work and see if we can find out where your colonel is hiding out. I want to meet this superstar."

34

Murph's Pub in Old Town Alexandria was crowded on this warm Saturday evening. There were many patrons that had to stand at the bar for lack of seating. But it didn't seem to bother them as they laughed and sang along with the Irish minstrel while drinking their Guinness and Irish whiskey.

Sean was extremely busy behind the bar and had no time to relax and talk to the customers. "Here's yah beer, mate. Cheers!" Sean said and began washing the cups and glasses then wiped off a corner of the bar.

Because of the crowd, Sean didn't notice the disheveled man entering the pub. Those standing near the door smelled the man before they even noticed him. Quickly, they distanced themselves from the stench.

The man was wearing a hooded sweatshirt in spite of the warm night temperature. The hood was pulled tightly over his head and his bearded face stared down at the floor as he stumbled while walking. The music was blaring, and the man stopped just behind those sitting on stools at the end of the bar.

A woman sitting at the bar gagged while pinching her nose as she whispered to Sean. "Damn, that guy standing behind me smells like shit. You need to kick him out before someone else does."

Sean quickly glanced beyond the woman and asked the man, "Ey, mate, what'll yah have?" If it be nothin' then move on outta here!"

The man didn't move but mumbled a response. Sean strained to hear over the loud music and laughter. So, he asked again, but this time with an edge to his voice and little diplomacy.

"Tell me what yah want to drink or buggar off!"

The man slowly raised his hood covered head and said, "Bourbon! JB Black straight up and make it a double."

Sean's head ratcheted upward.

"Oh, sweet mother of God, it be you, Mitch! Let me find yah a stool to rest your weary bones. I'm sure these fine folk will make room for yah at the end of the bar."

Sean found a stool and pointed for Mitch to sit. "It be sometime since I last saw yah. Please, my good friend, the first round be on me."

Sean ignored the nasty comments of the other patrons complaining about Mitch's filthy condition. "Buggar off," he told the woman. "This man is a war hero."

Sean leaned over the bar toward Mitch. "I read the tragic story about yah newspaper lass that was gunned down near Gadsby's Tavern. Bloody hell, Mitch, and that bastard that did it has not been caught. When will this all end for yah? Those bastards are relentless and seems they'll be continuing until they have achieved their goal. Which I believe is yah death!"

Sean placed the glass of bourbon on the bar in front of Mitch while others standing nearby grimaced and complained.

"No offense, barkeep, but your friend stinks. You need to kick his ass outta here or I will."

Sean leaned over the bar and got very close to the well-dressed man wearing a three- piece suit. His teeth were clenched, and his jaw tightened. "Listen, mate, yah have no clue what that gent has gone through. He be strugglin' with a number of serious issues. I suggest yah ease up on the lad. He be a close friend of mine. Besides, I'll determine whose arss will be kicked, and it won't be his or mine!"

Not wanting to draw attention to himself, Mitch slowly slipped off the stool and moved toward the door.

By the time Sean glanced at his friend, all he saw was an empty stool and a glass of bourbon. He quickly looked up and saw Mitch slowly walking out of the pub. Sean bolted over the bar just missing a few patrons and ran outside. He saw Mitch stumble and fall along the curb of King Street.

"Mitch let's return to Murph's so I can get yah a fine bowl of that Irish stew. It seems yah have gone too many nights without a good meal."

Sean helped him up and put his arm around Mitch's shoulder as they walked back into the pub. After he sat Mitch back on the stool, he caught the eye of a waitress.

"Be a darlin' and get me a nice bowl of that stew with a bit of bread and butter."

Mitch sat silently as if he was praying to his bourbon. His head was bowed, his hands cupped the glass of Kentucky magic, the hood of his sweatshirt still drawn. He knew that his life had hit rock bottom. Tears were running down his cheeks and onto the bar.

35

As the white sedan pulled into the parking lot, Rabah was distracted by a small corporate jet making a low pass over a nearby airfield. He parked the car as directed by Seth Hunt near a gray nondescript building along the Palwaukee Airport flight line in Wheeling, Illinois. Rabah noted that the airport was approximately twenty miles north of Chicago in the small town of Wheeling. There was very little activity, both in the air and on the ground, which seemed to please Hunt.

There were nineteen men waiting in the gray one room building that resembled a classroom with desks lined in rows. They had come from different regions of America but were citizens of the Mideast and North Africa. What linked them all was their common bond of faith in Islam, affiliation to the al-Qaeda, and undying allegiance to Osama bin Laden. As they waited many smoked and quietly spoke in Arabic.

Just before Hunt entered the building, he turned toward Rabah.

"You will wait outside and go nowhere. Regardless of the length of time I am inside this building you will not move. Do you understand?"

"Yes Master. I completely understand."

As Hunt entered the room all those within immediately stopped smoking and talking.

They stood at attention as if in the military. Hunt commanded them to sit as he stood on a small speaker's platform and looked down upon them as a tyrannical despot.

"*Assalam alaikum* my brothers of the al-Qaeda." Hunt paced, limping back and forth on the platform staring at each of the attendees.

"Warriors of the jihad, I have been directed to inform you that it is not by coincidence that you are here. Each of you was personally selected by our great leader, Osama bin Laden. As he stated, 'You represent the distinguished and honored tip of the Islamic spear that will impale the great Satan, America!' Now my brothers, you will carefully listen to what I have been commanded to tell you. It is the great leader's desire to bring our jihad to the streets and citizens of America. They have been sleeping as fat glutinous pigs in their capitalist shit for too long as the rest of the world suffers. It is time for their blood to pour through the streets of their villages, towns, and cities. I shall now explain in detail what Osama bin Laden demands of each of you."

- • - •

Rabah was leaning against the car as he took the last drag of his cigarette. There was a chill in the morning spring air, and he was worried about his wife and children. He had not communicated with them for some time, but he knew that defying Hunt would lead to his family's demise. He felt lost and began to pray aloud to Allah.

"Please protect my loved ones, Allah. They are innocent lambs that do not deserve to be led to slaughter. I don't know why you chose me to be with this madman, Hunt? He is a demon who will continue to kill until he has achieved his goals. I cannot remain with this tyrant. It is just a matter of time before he kills me. Help me, Allah, help me! Give me a sign, Oh Great One!"

As Rabah reached into his jacket pocket for his cigarette pack, the car keys dropped to the pavement. He stared in amazement at the keys and said, "Oh thank you, Allah!" Then he quickly picked them up, got into the car, and drove out of the parking lot heading southeast to DC.

36

After Abella's first month of living in the States, Mallory had finally convinced her that their search for Mitch was going nowhere, and they needed a break. So, each weekend they had pledged to go out and discover the DC nightlife. After exhausting most of the bars in Georgetown, they were now working on Alexandria.

"Abella, I can't believe that it's been weeks since you arrived. And still we've made little headway finding your colonel. On the other hand, we've gone to so many bars I've lost count. But what I really love about being with you is that I don't have to troll and work on getting guys' attention. Once they see you its nonstop free drinks, and all we have to do is listen to their BS. They continuously hit on you. But Abella, you've gotta lighten up. Please stop telling them to get the hell away. Believe me, they aren't all creeps. There were some great looking guys that probably would have taken us to dinner. I'm thinking that if this Mitch guy of yours really wanted you, he would have sent out an all-points bulletin to have you tracked down in Algiers or Paris. Now listen to me, there are two cute guys that keep staring at us at the other end of the bar. All we have to do is look over and smile. I guarantee they will be here in a heartbeat buying us drinks and maybe a bowl of that famous Irish stew. Now girlfriend, you've gotta get on with your life. With all that you've told me, you should feel lucky that you're still breathing. Hey, how about if I just wink at them?"

Mallory picked up her wine glass and was just about ready to send her signal to the guys when she was distracted.

"You know, Abella, it really pisses me off when I see a drunk in a decent establishment like Murph's! Do you see him at the end of the bar? He's the one wearing the dirty, ragged hoodie. Damn, he's so drunk he can't keep his head up and his face is practically kissing the bar. What a fucking loser! Why in the hell don't they throw him out of here?"

Abella had been staring into her wine glass while clutching the end of her necklace. Her mind was far away as she tightly held the ring that Mitch had given her during their last moments together in the Casbah. She felt the pain of loss in her heart and the tears in her eyes as she slowly looked up at what had disgusted Mallory.

— • — •

Sean placed the bowl of stew in front of Mitch and whispered, "Yah look rough mate. Please eat and sip yah bourbon. There's no need to leave. To hell with all the others."

Mitch looked up at Sean through bloodshot eyes. "Sean, I can't continue. I don't know where my life is going. Those that I cared for are gone. It's because of me they're no longer alive! Colleen is dead and Abella is a memory of love lost."

With that said Mitch took a long draw of his bourbon and lowered his head closing his eyes.

— • — •

"Please don't be angry at me, Abella. I gave those cute guys a big smile and now they're heading to our side of the bar."

Abella didn't hear Mallory; her mind was attempting to comprehend what her eyes had just seen. Through her tears she stared intently at the gaunt filthy man at the end of bar. There was something familiar about the way he raised his glass of bourbon. She noticed the soft blue color of his eyes, the blondish hair sticking out from the hood, and a scar on the left side of his forehead. She unconsciously tightened her grip on the ring.

As the two men approached the women with smiles and well-rehearsed pickup lines, Abella moved from her stool and walked slowly through the crowded pub trying to get a better look at the hooded man.

After serving drinks to a group near Mitch, Sean turned to his friend with a worried look. "Mitch, please take a spoonful of stew while it's hot. Yah need somethin' warm in yah belly."

Mitch looked up at Sean and nodded. Then he reached into his pocket and pulled out the long burgundy colored ribbon that still had a slight smell of jasmine. He held it close and cherished the fragrance while his mind drifted back to those wonderful moments in Algeria.

Then responding to Sean, he said, "Thank you for being so kind, but I must leave."

Abella froze when she heard the hooded man speak. It seemed a lifetime since she had heard that voice. She quickly moved and stood next to him as his head was bowed and his eyes closed. Then she saw her ribbon in his hand. Abella reached out and held Mitch's hand in hers.

"*Mitch . . . Mitch . . .* it's me, Abella." She choked back tears.

Mitch heard the tender voice, smelled the jasmine in her hair, and felt the gentle touch of her hand. He began to cry thinking that he was hallucinating. Mitch slowly opened his eyes and looked at his hand that was being held. Then he felt her dark black hair rub against his face as Abella leaned over and kissed him on the forehead. Mitch looked up and saw the full beauty of Abella standing inches away from him.

"Please tell me that I'm not dreaming. Please, Abella, tell me that you're really here and I'm not losing my mind."

As Mitch slowly stood from the stool, Abella wrapped her arms tightly around him and whispered. "It isn't a dream. I've finally found you and I'll never let you go away again."

37

Rabah pulled into the parking lot of his apartment in Springfield, Virginia and quickly entered the lobby. He took the stairwell running up to the second floor where he and his family lived. Abruptly entering his apartment, Rabah's wife and children were startled by his unexpected arrival. He didn't hesitate with formalities, but sternly directed his wife and children to pack.

"Quickly, pack only clothes and toiletry items. We must depart immediately!"

Rabah's wife was confused and could tell her husband was panic stricken. She stood shaking her head while looking perplexed.

"What is going on, Rabah? Why must we leave like this? What have you done?"

"I have no time to answer your questions. Just do as I say!" Rabah responded as he frantically stuffed clothes in a suitcase.

His two children began to cry, but he had no time to console them. He helped them pack and then they all quickly ran to the car and departed.

"Rabah, please tell me what has happened and where are we going?"

"It is that evil madman, Seth Hunt. The tyrant threatened to kill us if I did not do as he demanded. Now we are all in danger of losing our lives. I abandoned Hunt in Chicago. I do not regret my actions. I had begged Allah to help me, and he did. That is why I am here. You asked where we are going. First, you must understand that we cannot trust anyone. We cannot go to the mosque for help because his people there will kill us. We cannot go to the police because I fear that there are evil ones working for Hunt lurking among the authorities. I'm not sure where we are going, but we must leave quickly! I fear he and his evil followers will find us if we remain in our apartment."

"Rabah, what about all of our dreams and future plans for our children? Why has Allah allowed this to happen to us?"

"You must understand that it was Allah that gave me a sign to leave that psychotic Hunt in Chicago. Perhaps Allah will lead us to someone that we can trust to help us."

- • - •

As Rabah drove on the DC Beltway toward the Woodrow Wilson Bridge leading to Maryland, he asked his wife to open the glove compartment and remove a map of the state. As she opened the compartment a small piece of scrap paper fell landing near her feet. She picked it up and examined it.

"Rabah, what is this address? It is written not of your hand, but another's. It identifies a Christian church called Christ Church of Alexandria and says something about an old horse stable apartment."

Rabah immediately looked at his wife and said, "*Al hamdu lillah,* it is another sign from Allah. We are going to that location. As crazy as it might sound, that note is our only hope of salvation on this earth. We must find the one man that Seth Hunt fears the most."

"You are talking like a madman, Rabah. Stop this babbling in front of the children!" his wife pleaded.

"You don't understand my love, we must pray to Allah that Colonel Mitch Ross will understand our situation and forgive me for what I have done. If he does not pardon my transgressions, then surely he will attempt to kill me."

38

Abella helped Mitch from the taxi as he mumbled an apology about his Alexandria apartment. He pushed the door open and Abella gasped at the chaotic sight. Dirty clothes thrown about, remnants of moldy food, and countless empty bottles of bourbon littering the floor. Then while stepping into the semi-darkened apartment, she smelled a disgusting stink. She glanced into the bathroom noticing the unflushed toilet, ripped shower curtain, and broken mirror.

She grabbed Mitch and gazed into his eyes.

"Mitch, from what I could gather reading news accounts you have been through hell. And it's obvious that the effects have been extremely detrimental to your physical and mental health. But it hasn't been a cake walk for me either since we last were together! I've also experienced a hellish existence during this past year. But now that we're together I want us as it was before! Even if we must stay here in this one room apartment, we'll make it our home. I just hope and pray that you still love and want me?"

Mitch felt ashamed of his appearance, that of his apartment, and where his life had gone. He knew this was not how he had envisioned it would be meeting Abella again. He slowly reached out and took Abella's hand and kissed it.

"You asked if I still love and want you? When you stood near me in the pub, and I realized you were not an illusion. I knew my life was beginning again. I have never stopped loving you, Abella, and I never will."

Abella began to cry as she held him tightly and whispered, "I hope you have a lot of soap, a new razorblade, and a big garbage bag. Because it's going to take a long time to not only clean you up, but also this filthy apartment."

- • - •

While Mitch was in the shower, Abella, found a few large paper bags and began collecting the trash scattered throughout the apartment. She had already piled all of Mitch's dirty clothes in a corner and lined the empty bottles of bourbon along the wall near the front door. She pulled the covers from the couch cushions in anticipation of washing them as she glanced over at the small fireplace. Although the lighting wasn't good in the room, she immediately recognized the darkened silhouette of a handgun. Abella dropped the cushion covers and quickly moved near the object to confirm what her eyes had seen. She squatted to examine the 9mm pistol. Slowly and carefully, she picked it up and noticed that it was cocked. She released the clip from the grip and ejected the bullet. Abella gathered the clip and bullet along with the gun, placing them on the couch.

The bathroom door creaked as it slowly opened, and Mitch stepped out wearing his old Algerian robe. He no longer had a beard. And had made a poor attempt to trim his hair, which was now combed straight back off his face. Other than a few pounds lighter, he appeared to be the Mitch that Abella remembered.

"Hey, handsome! Now that's the man I fell in love with," Abella said as she grabbed the collar of his robe, stood on her toes, and kissed him.

"I wish I had a picture of how you're looking at me. It's truly a look of love. I see it in your eyes, in your smile, and the touch of your soft lips. I honestly thought I had lost you. I don't know why or how the stars perfectly aligned to guide you to Murph's tonight, but thank God our paths crossed." Mitch said as he held her tight and could smell the heavenly scent of jasmine.

There were no further words needed as they both had a burning desire to share their love. Mitch slowly began to remove Abella's blouse as she untied the soft terrycloth belt from his robe. Then as he guided her to the couch they were startled by a knock at the door. Abella looked at her watch and then at Mitch as she stood near the thick ancient door.

"So, do you normally have guests visit at one in the morning?"

Mitch moved Abella away from the door and looked toward the fireplace. Abella could see his perplexed look as he moved closer to that area of the room.

"If you're looking for your gun it's on the couch . . . unloaded," Abella fearfully said as she pointed where it rested.

Mitch quickly grabbed the gun, shoving the clip in the grip, and cocked the weapon. He firmly tied the belt which secured his robe then cautiously approached the door and said to

Abella, "Please move against the wall away from the door. Just in case this might be unpleasant."

Abella sadly looked at him and whispered, "Oh Mitch, when will this all end for us?"

Mitch partially pulled the door open and rapidly stepped back bringing the gun up to a firing position. As the feeble light from his apartment lit the darkness, he could see two young children standing on the doorstep. They screamed when they saw the gun pointing at them.

Abella yelled, "What is it, Mitch?" Then without thinking she ran to his side.

The mother stepped from the darkness, wrapping her arms around her crying children. As the chaos ensued Mitch noticed movement beyond the three, squinting to get a better look at a man who seemed strangely familiar. Then his mind rapidly recalled the evening Colleen was gunned down near Gadsby's Tavern. As Mitch stepped past the woman and children, the light from his room illuminated Rabah's face. *Seth Hunt's driver!* The man who had knocked him down as he was attempting to kill Hunt. Mitch pushed Abella back into the apartment as he pointed the 9mm at Rabah's face.

Rabah fell to his knees with head bowed and his hands raised as if in prayer. Then he screamed out in Arabic, *"Leysh, leysh min fudluk la, la!"*

Upon hearing the words that seemed so strange in America, Abella ran out the door grabbing Mitch's arm. "Mitch, please no! I don't know who this man is, but he is begging for his life. Please don't do anything that you'll regret. Please Mitch, I beg you! These are his children and wife."

"This son of a bitch was involved in the death of someone very dear to me."

"I know, it was Colleen." Abella said. "The reporter."

Mitch was stunned. *How the hell could Abella know anything about Colleen? How did she know her name?* Mitch slowly lowered the gun as Abella put her arms around the woman and children. She welcomed them into the apartment speaking Arabic to their surprise. *"Assalam alaikum,"* she said as she pushed the door wide open and beckoned them to follow. She turned to Mitch looking into his eyes, reached out and softly took the gun from his hand.

Rabah slowly stood, keeping his head bowed and walked past Mitch joining his family. Mitch turned to Abella and whispered, "How did you know about Colleen?"

"It's a long story, Mitch, and many articles read in the *Washington Post*. My old college girlfriend saved the stories about your exploits, and I spent many evenings reading them. I read about the tragic death of Colleen Duffy and your involvement, but they never caught the killer."

Mitch responded. "Not to alarm you, but this man assisted Seth Hunt in killing Colleen!"

Abella's head snapped up and she stared at Rabah. He could tell something was said about him that was not good and he began to frantically speak in English.

"I am not here to cause harm. I have brought my family to escape that madman, Ahmad Muhammad, or as you know of him as, Seth Hunt. He and his followers are searching to kill me and my loved ones—and they will not rest until you are dead, Colonel Ross. I abandoned him in a town north of Chicago where he was meeting with warriors of al-Qaeda. I fear they are preparing to strike and kill many Americans. He forced me to assist him under the penalty of death if I refused. I had no other recourse but to carry out his desires. You are the only one he truly fears in this world, and I believe you are the only one that can stop him. I will give my life to help you rid the world of this Satan. Please believe me!"

Rabah dropped to his knees again.

Abella reached into her purse for a chocolate bar as she explained in Arabic to Rabah and his family that she was from Algeria. She wanted to reassure them that their decision to find Mitch was the correct choice even though she was not convinced that Mitch believed Rabah.

When Mitch finished dressing Abella whispered to him, "In spite of what you might think, Rabah is truly sincere. I feel deep in my soul that he was not lying to us. I believe he will give his life to stop Hunt. But let's accommodate them as best we can. I don't think they have eaten for quite some time. I know it's so late, but is there any chance that we can get some food and drink for us all?"

Mitch glanced at his watch and noticed that it was almost two in the morning. "Damn, I don't have food in the house and Murph's closes in a few minutes. Let me run to the pub and see what I can come up with." Mitch grabbed his jacket and ran from the apartment into the darkness.

Within a few minutes he was entering the pub as the minstrel was announcing his last song.

"Jesus, Mary, and Joseph! Now there be the lad that I recognize. Look at yah, all shaved, combed, and cleaned! Not sure who that beautiful lass was that yah left with, but obviously she be a very good influence on yah!" Sean smiled. "Now what would bring yah back here at this time of the evenin', especially knowin' that there be that pretty thing waitin' for yah at the flat?"

"Sean, believe it or not somehow the good Lord brought Abella back into my life. That was her who pulled me out of the pub and cleaned me up. But that's not why I'm here. Is there any chance that I can order whatever you have left cooking in the kitchen? Abella and I had a few unexpected guests arrive, and they really need to eat."

"Well, I believe there be stew and some corn beef and cabbage. How about if I drop by yah flat in a few minutes once I get all the fixin's together."

"Sean, I can't tell you how much I appreciate this. How much do I owe you?"

"Listen my friend, this be my gift to yah and yah lady. Now I believe yah should get back to the flat and I'll be there soon with the food. But before yah go, here is a bottle of wine and container of coffee. Would there be anythin' else yah might need?"

"Maybe a little milk for the kids."

"Kids yah say? Hmmm, this be an interestin' get together at such a late night. Yes, here be the milk and I'll put it all in a sack for yah." Sean quickly gathered the drinks and Mitch was on his way back to the apartment.

Abella was still talking in Arabic to the family when Mitch returned. She quickly noticed that he only had drinks. "Mitch, where's the food?"

"Not to worry, sweetheart. Sean the bartender will be here shortly with the food."

Within a few minutes there was a knock at the door. Rabah and his family recoiled and huddled together anticipating the worst. Mitch went to the door and cautiously opened it. Sean was standing with his arms full of bags and a large grin on his face.

"Come on in, Sean, and let me introduce you." Mitch said.

Before Sean stepped into the room he leaned over and whispered while still grinning. "There be an interestin' occurrence in Murph's once yah left. I was gatherin' up the food when a fine lookin' lady approached me and asked about yah. She wanted to know if yah had said the name Abella. I responded affirmatively and she then asked if yah we're Colonel Mitch Ross? Now there be no one in the pub at that late hour knowing yah. So, I asked who she might be. She said that Abella be her old school friend who had deserted her earlier in the evenin'. So, Mitch, all I'm sayin' is that Mallory be an attractive caring lass and helped me tote the food for yah."

Mallory stepped from the darkness into the light with her arms full of bags of food.

Abella stepped to the door, and when she and Mallory saw each other they both joyously yelled out. Abella grabbed a few bags and took Mallory into the apartment completely ignoring Mitch and Sean.

The two men looked at each other and laughed. Rabah's wife, Abella, and Mallory collected the food along with the paper plates and plastic utensils. There was more than enough food and drink to go around.

As Mitch stood back in the room watching everyone enjoying their meal, the tension and stress suffocating him was gone. He smiled, reflecting on the evening and thought, *What began as an attempt to commit suicide has turned into a dream come true. Thank God Abella has reentered my life. Within hours she has miraculously transformed me to the person I was and given me a reason to live again.* He looked at Sean, who flashed him a thumbs up. Then he caught Abella's eye and smiled, noticing that she was helping the children with their dinner. While looking at the children, he saw a slight flicker of light near the front door and heard a whisper.

"Colonel, there is abundant joy and peace because she is here."

Mitch grinned and now knew what the ghost had meant earlier in the evening. He looked again at Abella and thought, *Yes, thank God, she is here.*

The ghost spoke again in a soft quiet voice that only Mitch could hear. *"Enjoy this happiness, colonel, for it is fleeting."*

39

The room in Wheeling fell silent as Seth Hunt prepared to continue his dictatorial rant about Osama bin Laden's plans against America. The al-Qaeda members in the room had just returned from a short pause allowing them to relax and smoke.

As they sat attentively waiting for Hunt to resume, one member entered and approached the speaker's platform seeking Hunt's attention. Hunt glared at the young man.

"What's so important that you must interrupt me and your fellow warriors?"

The young man bowed his head and replied, "I have something very important to tell you, master."

"You have something that is more important than my words? I will determine what is important! If I find it not worthy, I will personally punish you." Hunt leaned over and revealed a knife sheath attached under his trousers just above his right ankle. He withdrew the knife and stood. "Well now, begin your story my brave man!"

"Please, master, don't kill me! I'm not worthy of your punishment, but you must know that your driver is no longer in the lot waiting for you. He fled."

Hearing that Rabah had departed, Hunt stood stoically while firmly clenching the knife.

Hunt's face flushed a scarlet red. His eyes widened and his jaw clenched as he raised the knife above his head. Hunt took a step toward the kneeling man, wanting to bury the weapon deep into the whimpering target.

As others watched in horror, Hunt paused and slowly lowered the knife, containing his rage. He commanded the young man to rise.

"Stand my noble brother. You risked your life to tell me of the unpleasant situation that I now find myself. Although there are others in this room who undoubtedly observed my driver's departure, you were the only one brave enough and willing to inform me. For what you have done you will be rewarded. Your name will be sent to our leader honoring your bravery."

Hunt turned to the others who were still sitting attentively taking in every word as if Osama bin Laden himself was speaking.

"My brethren, it seems that we had a traitor among us." Hunt said in a calm, but direct voice. "My driver has betrayed our jihad, the al-Qaeda, and most importantly Osama bin Laden.

We cannot tolerate traitors! Therefore, once he is found there will be punishment. It will be a lesson to each of you to never betray the al-Qaeda and our mission.

"When he is captured, I will force Rabah to watch as I have his family mutilated. Their body parts will be thrown to rabid dogs! Then what I will do to Rabah will make him wish he had never existed on the earth. Once I have tracked down that pig, I will slowly behead him using a small paring knife. Then, my fellow al-Qaeda brethren, his severed head will be placed on the statue of Andrew Jackson in Lafayette Park across from the White House. A note will be stuffed in his mouth proclaiming our jihad. This will be done so all infidels will understand the power of the al-Qaeda!"

Hunt began to chant in Arabic over and over, *"Marg bar Āmrikāe. Marg bar Āmrikāe. Marg bar Āmrikāe."* Then he yelled in English raising the dagger above his head, "Death to America. Death to America. Death to America."

All those in the room began to raise their arms above their heads as they danced and chanted, *"Marg bar Āmrikā. Marg bar Āmrikā. Marg bar Āmrikā.*

40

Mitch and Abella struggled to determine where Rabah and his wife would sleep in the small apartment. It was almost four in the morning and Rabah's two children had long since fallen asleep on the couch. Mitch could tell that stress had taken its toll on Rabah as he was sitting on the floor leaning against the wall resting his head in the palms of his hands. Abella leaned toward Mitch and whispered as they were gathering the used plates and utensils from dinner.

"Mitch, do you have any idea where everyone will sleep? There's only the couch and the kids seem to have confiscated it for their bed."

"I notice that the youngsters look rather comfortable stretched out, but to answer your question, I'm clueless. I can't really insist that Sean take them home. His apartment is just a little larger than mine."

Sean and Mallory were laughing and flirting as they sat on the floor near the fireplace. They had been inseparable all evening. As they whispered and joked while sipping their wine, Mallory looked over at Abella and motioned for her to come over.

"It seems that our two love birds want a word with me. I'll be back in a second to try and solve our sleeping dilemma."

Mallory stood and wrapped her arms around Abella. "Hey girlfriend, tonight has turned into one of the best nights since we were in college. Sean is such a terrific guy and so damn funny. Plus, I love that Irish accent of his. But to change the subject, we noticed that the only people able to sleep in this flat are Rabah's kids. Sean and I laughed knowing that you and Mitch haven't had any private time together. So, I hope you don't mind, but we came up with a plan. You don't have to accept it, but it's at least a possible solution so that you two can catch up on a lot of lost time. You know, getting naked and playing grab ass! Sean has an old Plymouth minivan, and my apartment in Georgetown is much larger than this place. Plus, I have an ulterior motive to be honest with you. Sean has agreed to drive me and Rabah's family to my place, and maybe I can convince Sean to spend the night. I know what you're thinking, Abella! There's only about one to two hours remaining of the night, and Sean and I just met. But I gotta tell yah, there's a chemistry here that I've not felt in a long time. So just go with it, Abella. Sean will get his van and we'll haul ass to Georgetown while you two rekindle your relationship."

"Mallory, you and Sean are angels from Heaven. Mitch and I have been struggling with what we were to do about Rabah and his family. There is a lot I need to tell you about Rabah and why he's here. But for now, let's go with your plan. It will be safer and better for all of us if they stay in Georgetown. And by the way, a blind man could see and feel the chemistry between you and Sean. I'm so happy for you. But I better tell Mitch of the plan before he has a major migraine trying to come up with a sleeping solution."

Abella kissed Mallory on the cheek and caught Mitch's attention. Mitch quickly moved to where Abella and Mallory were standing. Before anyone spoke, Sean, who was still sitting on the floor with his wine, spoke up.

"Hey, why don't yah take a load off yourselves and join me on the floor. It be much more pleasant, and I won't have to arch me neck to look at yah." Sean then raised his wine glass as if toasting them all as they laughed and sat. "So, Abella, did yah fine lookin' girlfriend tell yah of our plan? I believe it'll work, and it be no disposition for me."

Mitch looked at Abella with a confused gaze. Abella reached out and held Mitch's hand.

"Sean and Mallory came up with a great solution to our problem.

Basically, Mallory will have Rabah and family stay with her in Georgetown. He needs to leave Hunt's car behind, so Sean will transport them in his van."

Mitch pulled Abella closer to him and whispered, "That, I believe, will solve something that's been gnawing at me all night. I'm sure Hunt's terrorist buddies would find an easy target if Rabah stayed here. It would be one stop shopping for those bad guys. They would take us out plus Rabah and family. But staying with Mallory in Georgetown will allow us time to figure out what to do in the long term. What I mean by that is working out something permanent for Rabah's safety. We also must go on the offensive and stop Hunt from doing whatever he's up to. But, Sweetheart, most important we need to get more one-on-one time together."

"I knew you would understand." Abella said as she kissed Mitch.

As Abella spoke in Arabic to Rabah and his wife of the plan, Sean and Mallory had departed for the van. Within thirty minutes Mitch and Abella were saying goodbye to their guests as they stood alone in the apartment.

"Well, Colonel, I believe the last time we were alone I had untied your belt, and you were removing my blouse. Even though it's practically morning, I'm game if you are?" Abella said with a flirtatious look.

Mitch smiled and said nothing as he began to remove Abella's clothes. She moved closer and slowly unbuttoned his trousers. Although there was a slight chill inside the cavernous room, they both began to feel the passionate heat of their love. As Mitch gazed upon Abella's naked beauty and felt an uncontrollable craving, she took his hand, and they moved toward the couch. Abella beckoned Mitch to join her as she raised her arms toward him. He softly rested on her as she whispered, "This moment reminds me of the first night that you and I were intimate at the embassy in Algiers."

Mitch smiled and then passionately kissed her as their bodies intertwined and their souls rejoiced in love.

41

The morning came too early for Mitch and Abella as they snuggled on the couch under a single blanket. Abella yawned and kissed Mitch on the forehead as he slept. He began to stir and slowly opened his eyes.

"You're here with me," Mitch said with a tone of surprise. "I thought I was still having the dream I've had since saying goodbye to you at the Casbah." He hugged Abella and kissed her.

She smiled and then asked, "So tell me, is there any possibility to make coffee in this stable?"

"Actually, there isn't too much here that can accommodate our basic needs. Sorry, sweetheart, but unless you want to drink the cold coffee that Sean brought from Murph's, we'll have to go out to get a cup of Joe and a bite to eat."

"Well, considering it's almost noon how about if we get cleaned up and go to a nice place that serves rich European coffee."

Mitch thought for a moment and then replied, "I know exactly where we'll go, and it overlooks the Potomac River adjacent to a small park. Really nice and there are usually sidewalk musicians along the wharf."

"That sounds great, Mitch! So, let's conserve time and water and squeeze into that shower together. By the way, if we're really considering on staying in this flat for an extended time, I need to speak to the owner! I think you've been too soft on the guy."

"Abella, in my defense I didn't anticipate staying here. I thought I would be destroyed by that Congressional Investigation Committee and sent to prison. So, in the meantime this place worked for me. But now that you're here, we can discuss changes to our living accommodations at brunch."

Once they were showered and dressed Mitch and Abella left the apartment and walked through the grounds of Christ Church. Mitch was unusually quiet.

"Is something bothering you?" Abella asked.

Mitch stopped and looked at Abella while standing near Major Richard Phillips headstone. "The last time I was standing in this cemetery I was talking to Colleen, and then moments later she was dead."

Abella pulled Mitch closer to her and said, "Terrorists have caused great pain and suffering in our lives. But what we must always remember is that had it not been for that terrorist stabbing you on the beach during the Hungarian reception, we would never have met." Mitch's thoughts quickly returned to that moment during the reception when a terrorist shoved a stiletto deep into his abdomen. He remembered slowly losing consciousness and his will to live. Then, eventually waking from the attack in the Algerian army hospital, he was being cared for by an extremely intriguing and beautiful nurse—Abella.

Mitch slowly smiled and kissed Abella. "You're right. So, let's enjoy what's left of the morning and go to the Nautical House."

- • -

Mitch took Abella's hand, and they walked through the old colonial village of Alexandria. But Mitch made sure that they didn't take the route that would have them pass Gadsby's Tavern where Colleen had been gunned down. That moment still pained Mitch greatly, and he could feel the rage of revenge rising in his soul.

- • - •

As Mitch and Abella approached the wharf along the Potomac, they could hear a violinist playing near sail boats moored along the dock. The soft music drifted along with the light breeze. A small group of people stood near the musician, taking in the wonderful moment of the late morning sunshine casting its rays on the slow-moving river.

A seagull swooped down on floating bits of bread that an elderly woman dropped into the water as she walked along the edge of the wharf. Abella gazed upon the scene and then smiled at Mitch.

"This is so romantic and something we could never have had in Algiers. Thanks for bringing me here."

"Perhaps you're right, but I'm really hungry, so let's climb the wooden steps and go into the restaurant. I believe it has that special coffee that you yearn for," Mitch said as he held Abella's hand.

The interior of the establishment resembled an old sailing galleon with its tarnished brass nautical gear and scrimshaw carvings. There were large harpoons hanging from the parched wooden walls and paintings of four masted sailing ships long since gone from the seas. The main dining room was fashioned after the deck of an old wooden whaling vessel. A portion of the floor was elevated where the stern would have been located. The tables were spaced for privacy along with dimmed candle lighting. The side of the restaurant facing the Potomac was a wall of glass, allowing those sitting near a spectacular view of the river and any maritime traffic.

Mitch pointed to the glass wall and the receptionist led them to a small intimate table for two. Abella blushed as they were seated, and she leaned toward Mitch.

"Had I known it was to be this nice I would have stepped up my apparel. But considering all my clothes are still at Mallory's apartment these jeans and blouse will have to do."

Mitch laughed. "You look beautiful wearing anything. Let's enjoy the moment and have a cup of that rich coffee that they just poured for us."

The warmth of the sun shining through the window made their corner table cozy and intimate. As Abella and Mitch sipped their coffee and gazed out onto the Potomac she whispered, "Sorry to ruin this moment, but I really need to get to the ladies room."

"Not a problem, sweetheart. It's in the bar. Just walk near the front door and you'll see the bar."

As Abella walked into the bar, she heard a voice that caused her to immediately stop.

"Sweet Lord! Eitha the vodka in this Bloody Mary is causin' me to hallucinate, or my old, tired eyes are truly lookin' upon that beautiful angel from Algiers!"

Abella took a few steps backward.

"Jake! Jake it's you!" Abella screamed as she jumped into his arms. The tears began to stream as the big man spun her around as if they were dancing.

Jake lowered Abella back to the floor and with a wide grin said, "There's only one human being on this old earth that you would travel halfway around the world to see. It's been a while since I talked to the colonel. Let's go find him."

Abella's mind raced back to the Casbah remembering the last time she was with him. She truly thought Jake was dying in her arms after he had been severely wounded by the attacking terrorists.

"Jake, I can't believe you're alive! Mitch and I finally found each other last night and I haven't been able to ask him about you. What a great surprise!" Abella gave Jake another hug and then pulled him to the dining area where Mitch sat.

42

The sun glistened on the large lake that was nestled in the tree covered hills of Fontana, Wisconsin. It had once been the playground for Chicago's wealthy upper class. Their mansions still encircled the lake, although their owners had long since passed on.

Hidden in the trees along the western bank of the lake near the small town of Fontana, was a remote cabin, a perfect getaway for weekend fishermen or boaters. But now the only inhabitants were three men. Seth Hunt limped as he paced back and forth in the main room of the cabin as the two Algerians sat and listened.

"I have been told by informants in the DC area that my former driver's car was parked near the residence of a man that I hate and want dead. I have also been informed that his lady from Algeria is now staying with him."

Hunt pulled a map from a notebook lying on a small wooden table in front of the couch where the men were sitting. He spread the map and pointed to the location of Christ Church in Alexandria. Then he resumed pacing.

"You will note that Rabah's car was seen parked near the church. My informants have not seen him or his family. They searched his apartment in Springfield, Virginia but it was empty. They're obviously in hiding. But I want them found, tortured and killed."

Hunt paced some more, trying to control his rage.

"You are probably wondering why I'm staying in this cabin and not attempting to track down and kill Rabah and Colonel Ross, myself. This location is perfect for me at the present time. It affords me the opportunity to travel undetected to the training site of the jihadist warriors in Wheeling, Illinois. Once the training is complete, we will wait for our leader, Osama bin Laden, to confirm the timing of our attack.

"Also, you are aware that I killed a young female journalist in Alexandria. I am not concerned with that because I know if Ross should identify me as the killer, my Islamic warriors within the police force will intervene and kill any investigation. By the time the truth of her murder surfaces years will have passed, and I will have safely returned to Algeria. Rabah knows of my al-Qaeda contacts within the police department therefore I have directed that they track him down and kill him.

"I am sure you are quite confused at the moment, which is why I requested that you join me today. Now listen very carefully. There is a black van parked behind this cabin. You two will use it to travel to the DC area. Within the van you will find two handguns, rope, and tape. Your mission will be to find Colonel Ross and his woman, Abella. Once you have accomplished that you will restrain Ross and kidnap the woman."

Hunt became animated, his eye bulging.

You will NOT kill Ross under any circumstances. DO YOU UNDERSTAND! You will NOT kill him. You may injure him, but only to weaken him so that when he comes here, I can slay him like a matador slaying a weakened bull. The privilege of the kill is reserved for me. Do you understand?"

The men nodded fearfully.

"You will return to this cabin with the woman. She will be my bait to lure Ross. He will travel to the ends of the earth to rescue her. It will be like a rat mindlessly following the smell of the cheese, but not realizing he has entered the trap. I will relish that moment knowing the last thing the colonel will see, before I kill him, is his lovely lady tied up naked in this cabin."

"If something goes wrong while you are attempting to kidnap Ross's lady, here are two small containers that represent your escape. Each contains a cyanide capsule. You will take it if you are captured. I am sorry, but I cannot completely trust you from telling the authorities of this plan. Therefore, you will immediately take the capsule and your families in Algeria will be told that you died heroes of the jihad. They will be protected and taken care of financially. If I discover that you failed in your mission and were captured, you will wish that you were never born, and your families will be murdered. That is all I will say about that other than DON'T FAIL!"

After yelling the final two words, Hunt handed the containers of cyanide to each man. Then he grabbed a folder that had been resting on a counter in the kitchen.

"Within this folder are pictures of Ross and his woman. You will note that she is quite attractive, which will make your kidnapping of her much more pleasurable. There are also pictures and the address of Ross's flat near the Christ Church in Alexandria. Additionally, I have included pictures of Rabah, my former driver. If you should see him, kill him immediately, and his family if they are with him. That will definitely be a bonus gift for me. In fact, kill him and take photos using this camera."

Hunt handed over the camera, which had been on the table near the couch, and placed the photos back in the folder.

"You will leave immediately! The keys are in the van. Do not return unless you have Ross's woman. Do you understand?"

The two men stood bowing their heads. "Yes, Master, we understand completely and will carry out the orders as you have described. *Allah Akbar, Allah Akbar!*"

Hunt sat down on the couch and began to read the Koran while sipping cool tea. He paused while reading and began to laugh. He was thinking of how Ross would react seeing Abella naked in the cabin.

43

Mitch cleared the DIA headquarters security entry procedures and calmly waited for Admiral Scott's secretary to inform him that he could see the director. He was lost in thought reflecting back to when he had stood in the exact spot in the admiral's office weeks earlier. The last time he was here Colleen had just been murdered. *That bastard Hunt is somewhere in the States planning to ultimately kill more Americans, and me. I've gotta stop him!*

The nightmarish thoughts continually haunted Mitch and he knew that it would never end until he or Hunt was dead. But there was another dilemma that Mitch was struggling with. Whether or not to inform the admiral that Hunt was in the United States. The office door opened, and the director walked over to Mitch and shook his hand.

"Colonel Ross, you look a helluva lot better than the last time I saw you. Come on into my office and let's talk about what I want you to do for me here in the DIA. Do you need a cup of coffee?"

The admiral's casual approach took Mitch by surprise, and it made him feel quite awkward. "No, no thank you, sir. I'm just fine at the moment."

"Well, I hope you'll feel the same way after we talk. I know I said earlier that you needed to rest, but something has come up, and I need your help," the admiral said with a slight smile as he sat behind his large desk and motioned for Mitch to take the nearest leather chair.

Admiral Scott momentarily stared at Mitch as if he was analyzing his thoughts. "There is definitely a noticeable change about you. The last time we met you looked like you had just been kicked in the gut by a mule. But now you look much healthier and happy."

"Yes, sir. The time away was very good."

"Great! I'm glad to hear that, colonel. Now let's discuss something that I'm very much concerned about.

"Operatives in Algeria and Paris informed our agency that the terrorist Seth Hunt left Algiers sometime in December of last year. We now know that he traveled through Charles de Gaulle International and arrived in Washington. Unfortunately, his trail has grown cold and there has been no updates of his whereabouts. But what we do know from sources in the Middle East is that Osama bin Laden is planning something. Exactly what it is remains a mystery at this point, but I have a feeling Hunt is part of the plan. I'm working closely with the FBI to track Hunt down. If we find him, I believe we'll discover what bin Laden is up to. But this is what you, colonel, must understand. Under no circumstances will you get involved in anything dealing with Hunt from this point on. That is a direct order from me to you!" The admiral paused while staring at Mitch to emphasize what he had just said.

"We know that you are a very large target as far as Hunt and his terrorist buddies are concerned, because of your actions in the Casbah. It was probably Hunt or his cronies who attempted to kill you on two occasions of which we are aware. Therefore, I discussed with my counterparts at the FBI whether to use you as bait to draw Hunt out. But it was determined that would be too risky and more than likely result in your death. Thus, the order for you to stand down. Do you understand?"

Mitch was reluctant to answer the admiral but had no other recourse and responded affirmatively. "Yes, sir. I understand completely."

The admiral shifted in his chair and smiled. "Fine. Now that we're in agreement I'll tell you what your job will be here at the DIA."

- • - •

The weekend couldn't come fast enough for Mitch. His new job at the DIA basically consisted of babysitting a team of seasoned intel analysts. Their task was to update the annual DIA fact book. Mitch was well aware that the classified information inside the book was top secret. And he knew it was used extensively by members of the DIA when researching the military capabilities of countries. But the members of his team had accomplished this task for many years, so there was very little supervision needed. He would be relegated to sitting in his office drinking coffee while gazing out of a small window at buildings on Bolling Air Force Base.

These analysts are on automatic pilot, Mitch thought. *The real reason I've been assigned this do-nothing desk job is so that the admiral and DIA can keep tabs on my whereabouts. I believe he doubts my word that I'll obey his order to stand down. Well maybe there's some truth to that.*

44

Mitch rolled over and reached for Abella, unfortunately all he got was a handful of bed sheets and blankets. She had been up for at least an hour taking a shower and preparing breakfast as best she could with what she had in the small apartment. Abella had attempted to make the flat a little more livable, buying a toaster, coffee maker, portable clothes rack, and by doing a complete cleaning of the main room and bathroom.

Mitch could smell the wonderful aroma that only comes from a freshly brewed pot of coffee. Slowly and magically the percolator changed the cool clear water into a hot liquid breakfast. But as tempting as it smelled, the coffee would not be the foremost item he would crave this morning.

Mitch slowly opened his eye that wasn't buried in a pillow and could see the partially naked body of a beautifully tanned woman. The well-worn blue T-shirt she was wearing barely covered her athletic backside. As she reached over to place a slice of bread into the toaster, the tee rose to her waist and completely revealed her nakedness.

"Sweetheart, one of these days you're going to give me cardiac arrest as you walk around half naked while I'm trying to wake up. Talk about jumpstarting my heart in the morning!"

Mitch said smiling as he slowly sat up in bed and watched her glide effortlessly around the kitchen. He knew the coffee would be great, but what he really desired lay beneath the blue T-shirt.

"Sorry, but this T-shirt was the first thing I grabbed after getting out of the shower. I thought you would like how the color of the shirt matches my eyes." Abella laughed and winked at Mitch while putting the mugs of coffee and toast on a tray.

"To be honest, I didn't notice the color of the T-shirt. Now I'm wondering if I really need the coffee considering my libido has shifted into overdrive." Mitch reached and almost fell out of bed while attempting to pull Abella's shirt above her waist.

"Hey . . . hey, let's save that for later. You promised me that I would get a personal tour of downtown DC today. So, let's have a quick breakfast in bed and minimize the hanky-panky. We gotta get going so I won't miss anything," Abella said as she handed the tray of coffee and buttered toast to Mitch while sliding under the sheets next to him.

Mitch quickly drank his coffee and stuffed a piece of toast into his mouth. Then just before he jumped out of bed to get into the shower, he softly and slowly moved his hand touching her intimately. She closed her eyes, pressing her pelvis against his hand, and moaned. Then, Mitch jumped out of bed.

"Sorry sweetheart, but times a wasting, and you did say to minimize the hanky-panky. Plus, it's a little payback for your burlesque show while preparing breakfast."

45

A black van slowly drove from the banks of the Potomac River on a westerly heading along King Street. The driver slowed to pick up a man that was dressed as if he was to attend a sporting event. His black ballcap was pulled tightly over his head and his sunglasses concealed any facial identity. His red tee with long sleeves covered his dark complexion.

"*Sadam, as-salam alaykum,*" he said to his partner. "But here in America we must use their native tongue and say peace be upon you! My eyes are extremely tired from the hours of reading the ancient headstones in the cemetery of Christ Church while waiting for the imbeciles to depart. The infidel colonel and his Algerian bitch have finally left their flat and are walking on King Street. I suspect they are heading toward the metro station. Drop me off at the station and I'll take the same train that they select. Then you will drive into DC, and I'll keep you updated by phone on my location.

"It appears by their dress that today will be quite casual.... But there will be no moments of casual relaxation for them once we strike! I will follow the orders of our beloved leader, Ahmed Muhammad, and not kill Colonel Ross, but he said nothing of wounding him. I believe the beating I will inflict upon him will be unrecoverable. Then our leader can put him out of his misery with a well-placed bullet."

Mitch and Abella waited on the raised platform for the train to arrive that was heading into DC. They seemed oblivious to all that was going on around them and preferred to concentrate on each other as they softly spoke and kissed from time to time. The terrorist positioned himself behind a large ground-level billboard train schedule and a group of businessmen. But he remained close enough that he was able to monitor Mitch and Abella's every movement.

As the cars of the train arrived, passengers clustered by each entry door. The robotic announcement stating that the train was to depart in five minutes was the cue for the automatic doors to open as passengers rushed in to find available seating. Mitch and Abella calmly stepped into a car and were fortunate to find seats. They slowly sat while still holding hands, deep in conversation.

The terrorist entered and stood at the rear of the same car. He reached up and grabbed a leather loop to hold for balance, maintaining visual contact with Mitch and Abella.

"So, mister tour guide, are you always this friendly and loving to all your customers?" Abella jokingly asked as she nestled her head on Mitch's shoulder.

Mitch laughed. "I reserve that treatment exclusively for Georgetown University graduates who are French Algerian. Especially if they have traveled halfway around the world to spend time with a crazed American Air Force colonel!"

Abella smiled and raised her head from his shoulder and kissed him lightly on the cheek just as the announcement was made that the train was approaching Lafayette Station.

"Abella, this is where we get off." Mitch said as he carefully stood, bracing himself so as not to stagger while helping Abella.

The commuter train slowed as it approached the Lafayette Square Station, which was just a few blocks from the White House. As the doors opened, Abella and Mitch quickly departed and headed to Lafayette Square. They leisurely walked down Vermont Avenue enjoying the warm summer morning and entered the famous park dedicated to the young Frenchman who helped America win its independence. Mitch wanted to begin their day at the park because of its location just across Pennsylvania Avenue from the White House.

"Mitch, do you think the president is in the White House this morning?" Abella asked as she waved at the building as if President Bush was looking at her through a window.

"Not sure. But then again, I haven't been in the Oval Office to talk to him this week." Mitch laughed and reached for Abella's hand as they walked near the statues in the park."

"So, all these statues in the park are of General Lafayette?"

Mitch smiled. "No sweetheart, only one. Most people miss it because it's jammed in the southeast corner of the park."

Abella looked at Mitch and shook her head. "I don't understand why America names a park after a famous French general and he's stuck in the corner. In Algeria, when we name a park after a famous person their statue is in the center and is the ONLY statue in the entire park."

Mitch laughed again "You've got a good point there my dear. But here in DC there are so many statues and so little space. Let's walk over and I'll show you Lafayette. Then we'll cross Pennsylvania Avenue and take a closer look at the White House."

As they turned to walk toward Lafayette's statue, Abella noticed old row houses near where they had originally entered the park.

"Mitch, could we walk over to those beautiful old buildings before visiting the statue and the White House? I love colonial architecture. It reminds me of the small row houses I saw in Paris while walking near Yves's apartment.

"Of course we can. Today is your day and I'm your personal

guide," Mitch said as they turned from Pennsylvania Avenue and headed toward the old houses just northwest of the park.

As they approached a large brick building on H Street, Mitch noticed a small brass plaque just adjacent to the front door.

"I'll be damned! Abella, this might seem rather strange, but this house belonged to a man that has had a direct impact on your life. The special ring that you wear on the necklace. The ring that I gave to you when I said goodbye during those last tragic moments together in the Casbah. That ring was worn by the man that had this house built near the White House in 1818."

"What? How could a man living in Washington DC in the eighteen hundreds misplace his ring in Algiers? Then two hundred years later you find it at a jewelry shop in the Casbah. Mitch, that story seems a little farfetched!"

"Sweetheart, it's a long story, but I gotta say that it's completely factual. Oddly enough, the owner of this house was a famous naval officer. He had the house built with the money Congress gave him for his naval exploits in the Barbary Wars in North Africa and the War of 1812. Let's go inside and I'll explain why he had that Bedouin Sheik's ring."

As they entered the three-story colonial brick home, Abella was still baffled by Mitch's comments. "Why did you say that you thought that stumbling upon this house was strange?"

"It's just that I knew very little about the naval officer prior to our failed attempt to rescue Captain Seth Hunt. But the famous American has since become part of our lives. It was the elderly Algerian jeweler in the Casbah who explained to me how the young American obtained the ring. After fighting and killing the leader of the Barbary Coast pirates that were attempting to destroy the American naval vessels, the American pulled the ring from the dead Bedouin's finger. It is said that he wore the ring until his untimely death from wounds received in a duel. Somehow the ring found its way back to its origin, Algeria, and eventually the jewelry shop in the Casbah. What seems to be strange is that everyone who wore the ring met an early and tragic death. The jeweler in the Casbah never wore the ring. But that curse will not continue because I will not allow anything to happen to you. That ring was destined to be the symbol of my love for you, and it will always represent that as long as I'm living and breathing on this earth."

Abella clutched the ring that hung from the golden necklace around her neck. She pulled Mitch closer while standing on the stairs, kissing him passionately. Then she took Mitch's hand, and they climbed the stairs to the second floor.

The house had been decorated as it was when the naval officer and his wife entertained the Washington elite. Mitch walked across the large room to examine an old wooden desk with nautical memorabilia that the officer acquired throughout his career. Abella was looking at a table setting that had been arranged as if a large banquet dinner was to be served. As she examined the fine china and silverware, her gaze moved to an accompanying wall. Her demeanor immediately changed as she froze and gasped looking upon a larger-than-life portrait of the famous commodore standing in his naval dress uniform. The painting was at least nine feet tall, and she noticed the relatively young man peering out at her. Abella was hypnotized by his gaze, and as she stepped closer, in awe how authentic he seemed. Then her eyes widened as she subconsciously clutched her ring. There in the painting on Commodore Stephen Decatur's right middle finger was her ring. The ring he had taken after killing the pirate during their hand-to-hand combat in 1804.

Abella stumbled while stepping backward, reaching out to steady herself on the corner of the huge wooden dining table. She could barely speak as her eyes remained locked onto Decatur's hand that wore the ring.

"Mitch . . . Mitch, he's wearing my ring!"

- • - •

The terrorist had been watching and listening to Mitch and Abella as he sat on a park bench in Lafayette Square feeding squirrels with breadcrumbs. He observed them crossing the street and eventually entering Commadore Decatur's home. He waited a few minutes and then made a phone call to his driver, Sadam, to park the van on H street near the famous naval officer's brick house. He threw the remaining crumbs at the squirrels and slowly walked to the door of Decatur's home. Pausing, he cautiously looked for any tourists who might be approaching. But to his satisfaction, H street was unusually quiet for a summer morning in September. He entered the historic house and made little to no noise. The terrorist quickly surveyed each room on the first floor. The rooms were empty except for antique furnishings. Then he heard voices that he recognized coming from the second floor.

Slowly he withdrew brass knuckles from his trouser pocket and positioned them on his lefthand. He began to smile thinking of the impending beating of Colonel Ross. Next, he squatted and lifted his left trouser cuff revealing a small leather pouch attached just above his ankle. He slowly unsnapped the top and removed a small aerosol container of pepper spray. The terrorist put the container in his right trouser pocket and carefully proceeded up the steps to where the voices had been heard.

As he entered the second floor's large room, he noticed Abella and Mitch softly whispering and staring at Decatur's picture. They had their backs to him, and he wasted little time and quietly positioned himself within a few feet behind them. He slowly removed the pepper spray container from his trouser pocket and held it at eye level.

"*As-salam alaykum,* Infidels!" the terrorist boldly yelled.

Mitch and Abella practically jumped with fearful surprise while turning around to see who had made the menacing Arabic statement. Before they could react, pepper spray splattered into their faces and immediately rendered them defenseless. They both staggered while attempting to rid their eyes of the excruciating pain. Abella slammed into the large dining room table and fell to the floor screaming in agony. Mitch was still staggering around the room sightless while struggling to get to Abella. Then he felt a tremendous blow to his stomach as if being struck by a metal bat. Mitch dropped to his knees withering in pain clutching his abdomen. Abella was still screaming from the agony of the spray and the fear of the unknown.

Sadam had been calmly sitting in the black van outside of Decatur's home smoking when he was startled hearing Abella's screams. He immediately opened the center console of the van and removed a small two shot derringer and a roll of duct tape, then ran into the house. Upon entering the second-floor room he saw his colleague eager to smash Mitch's face with the brass knuckles.

Sadam yelled out in French to stop, *"Arret ... arret!"*

The terrorist immediately dropped his fist and looked surprised. Sadam ran to Abella withdrawing duct tape and used it on her mouth and around her wrists.

Abella attempted to scream out for Mitch as Sadam forcefully dragged her toward the staircase. The other terrorist kicked Mitch violently in the back then ran to assist Sadam.

As Mitch lay prone on the floor, his eyes were beginning to make out shadowy figures. He saw three murky shapes struggling near the stairs. He sprang from the floor and ran toward them. Sadam, seeing Mitch coming, quickly pushed Abella in the direction of the staircase. Instinctively she raised her tapped hands unable to grab the handrail. Abella lost her balance and fell headlong down the flight of steps.

Sadam yelled to the other terrorist to get Abella into the van. Instinctively he sidestepped Mitch's attack. Turning quickly, he pressed the derringer into Mitch's forehead and ordered him to stop resisting. Then he swiftly raised his knee and smashed it into Mitch's groin.

Mitch cried out from the overwhelming pain as he collapsed onto the floor in a fetal position. Sadam quickly ran down the steps and out the front door. Arriving at the black van he assisted his partner heaving Abella into the cavernous back cargo area of the vehicle. Sadam rapidly taped her ankles and then climbed into the driver's seat, speeding away on the DC Beltway while his colleague unfolded the roadmap.

46

Mitch slammed his fist against the old wooden wall of his Alexandria apartment. He yelled out in pain and cursed himself for being so inept. But the tremendous anger and agony that rose within him was because of the loss of Abella. Again!

"Ahh! How could I be so fucking stupid to let this happen. Why wasn't I more vigilant! Again, I've lost Abella and it's my damn fault!"

Mitch grabbed items in the living room, smashing them and throwing their remnants against the walls. After what seemed to be hours, he collapsed face down on the couch, sobbing uncontrollably on the verge of a nervous breakdown.

The flat was beginning to darken as very little of the sunset entered the old stable. Mitch felt overcome with fatigue, pain, and bewilderment. It had replaced his rage. He gradually rolled onto his back, and a soft light flickered near the fireplace. Mitch rubbed his eyes, and the light became brighter.

Major Phillips was standing and gazing at Mitch. Then the apparition spoke. "She lives, Colonel. Go to a lake the Potawatomi call Kishwauketoe. There is a small cabin west of the lake. She is there. Go quickly as the wind but beware the evil one is waiting."

As quickly as the ghost had appeared it vanished. Mitch was stunned and confused by what he had just heard. He kept thinking of the strange terms, *Potawatomi and Kishwauketoe.*

What the hell is he telling me? What does this shit mean? Then Mitch screamed out to the ghost.

"You can't just give me all this bullshit and expect me to know where the hell Abella is.

There's no time for guessing games!"

Mitch waited for a response, but there was none. He frantically grabbed a piece of paper, a pen, and wrote what he thought were the two odd sounding words spoken to him by Major Phillips. Mitch again began to speak to no one but himself.

"Where the hell can I go to find out the meaning of these strange words? Hopefully, they will reveal the location where Abella is being held. If I knew where the library was located in this town, at least that would be a beginning, but I have no clue where it's at."

As his mind filled with confused thoughts, he felt lost and saddened. Then Mitch's body was overcome with an extreme chill and a riveting mental image of a minuscule colonial bookstore on King Street near Murph's Pub.

What the hell, Mitch thought. *I've walked that street many times and don't recall seeing a bookstore near Murph's! Why do I get the impression that it's that damn ghost sending me these thoughts.*

Mitch squeezed the note he had written just moments before into the palm of his hand and ran out of his flat heading toward King Street.

– • – •

The old stone building was no larger than a two-room shed. Mitch noticed a small wooden sign commonly used during the colonial era resting on an ancient stool for all customers to see. Mitch slowly read the weathered markings etched into the wood and said them aloud, "Samuel Drake's Bookstore established 1751."

If this bookstore was established before the Revolutionary War, why the hell haven't I ever noticed it? Mitch thought as he felt a cold chill.

The old floor creaked as Mitch walked into the darkened room of dusty books and broken shelves. Then out of the darkness a frail voice spoke out startling Mitch.

"Can I be of service to you, young man? Mr. Drake is currently not here," a thin, elderly white-haired woman asked as she peered over her bifocaled glasses and rose from a well-worn rolltop desk. Mitch noticed that she was wearing an ankle length dress that hugged tightly around her neck, accentuating her frailty and stooped posture.

"Excuse me for being a little confused regarding your Mr. Drake comment, but I'm in somewhat of a rush and need help determining a location that is defined by two words," Mitch said while still questioning whether he was experiencing reality or fantasy while standing in the poorly lit musty room.

The old woman raised her glasses and positioned them above her forehead in her thinning white hair. "And what two terms might they be?"

Mitch glanced at the note he was still clutching and blurted out, "Potawatomi and Kishwauketoe."

The woman paused then responded, "Interesting that you mentioned those words. We used them in the early and mid-eighteenth century." She slowly turned away and returned to the rolltop desk.

"Aren't you going to help me?" Mitch blurted.

The woman chuckled upon hearing the tone of desperation in Mitch's voice.

"I am assisting you, young man. Please have patience."

She slowly reached up and opened a small drawer of the rolltop desk. Carefully, she removed a few old documents. Unfolding one of them, she lowered her glasses from the crown of her head and peered at the faded writing. After a moment she rose from the desk and slowly walked to a group of dusty, well-worn books leaning awkwardly on an uneven shelf.

"Yes, here it is," she whispered.

Mitch quickly moved near her as she opened the small, aged book that seemed not to have been touched for over a century.

"Hmmm . . . here is a reference to the word *Kiswauketoe*. This is quite interesting. It is an old term used by the Potawatomi tribe of Wisconsin. It loosely translates to clear water or lake of the sparkling water."

"Excuse me, but I don't care about those translations! Can you please tell me where exactly that clear water sparkling lake is located?"

The woman broke her hypnotic gaze from the page of the old book and glanced at Mitch. "You seem to be quite anxious to know what all this means as if a life depends on the answer. Or more specifically her life." The elderly woman paused staring into the darkness slowly nodding as if she knew exactly why Mitch had entered the bookstore. Mitch's head snapped up as he looked directly at her and was about to comment on her previous statement, but she ignored him and continued.

"The book mentions that the Potawatomi tribe lived in southeastern Wisconsin until 1836 when they were ordered out by the US government. They were forced to leave and escorted by the Army. Then the lake was renamed what we know it today, Lake Geneva. The Potawatomi left their sacred grounds never to return. It is also written that those sacred grounds are now a small village called Fontana."

Mitch's eyes widened when he heard the names that unlocked the mystery of Abella's location. Without thinking or saying a word, Mitch leaned over and kissed the old woman on the forehead. He dashed from the cold small bookstore heading toward Murph's Pub.

47

The rich aroma of tobacco and soft smokey haze encircled those that were browsing in the small, enclosed shop on King Street. The unique airborne elements from the John C. Tobacconist shop seemed to enrich the conversations as the patrons carefully examined the international selection of cigars.

An extremely large man was casually leaning against an old wooden bureau within the shop while chatting with a young woman who happened to be the manager of the establishment known as, The John C. Tobacconist of King Street.

"You know young lady, I've been smoking cigars longer than you've been on this planet. But I would never have taken a delicate graceful woman, that you are, to be such an aficionado of the fine aspects of tobacco. I thought I knew every detail about a Cohiba, but in the last thirty minutes you have graced me with your abundant knowledge of the finer aspects of this Cuban masterpiece."

Jake paused for a moment as he lovingly looked at his cigar and didn't notice the manager blushing from his compliments.

"To be honest, Mr. Davis, I always enjoy our conversations when you visit the shop. Your travels throughout the world and cigar knowledge are extremely fascinating. But please let's be less formal and call me by my first name, Janet, and not Miss Gamble."

Jake looked up and smiled, then reached into the inner breast pocket of his jacket and gave Janet a beautiful pristine Cohiba. She looked rather stunned and slowly took the rare Cuban gift. She held it in the palm of her hand as if it was a fragile ice sculpture.

"It's the least I can do, considering that it's been years since I lived in the DC area. Now, I have so few friends and acquaintances here. So, call me, Jake, and let's celebrate by lighten up. There's somethin' magical bout smokin' a quality cigar that feels and tastes like uncorkin' a fine wine."

"Thank you so much, Jake. This is truly a rare gift that I'm ready to enjoy. So as you light up let me quote Mr. Mark Twain who once said, 'If I cannot drink bourbon and smoke cigars in Heaven then I shall not go!'"

Jake laughed as Janet reached into her apron pocket and retrieved a small guillotine cigar cutter. As she carefully examined the head of the cigar, Janet's attention was instantly gripped by the sound of squealing tires, a sickening cry of someone injured, and the crash of a vehicle into the building adjoining Janet's tobacco shop.

Janet dropped the guillotine cutter and cigar while reaching up and grabbing Jake's large forearm for support. Jake had ducked and taken a few steps toward the door as his special agent training began to take over his thoughts and actions. He turned to Janet and quickly said, "Little lady, I believe you should stay put because I have a strange feelin' this might be more than just a pedestrian bein' struck by an auto."

Janet released Jake's arm, but as he rapidly opened the door and moved to a position near the disabled car, he noticed she was still glued to his side.

Janet stared at Jake with wide fearful eyes and nodded as she tightly grabbed a corner of his extremely large jacket.

Jake peered into the burning car and could see the driver slumped over the steering wheel. He quickly opened the passenger door, reaching across with his large arms unbuckled the seatbelt, pulling the man out. Jake lay the unconscious driver on the sidewalk.

But while doing that, something odd caught Jake's attention. It was a small unique tattoo on the palm of the man's left hand. As his thoughts began to drift back to Algeria, he refocused and yelled to bystanders to call 911.

Jake and Janet began to move toward the street where the pedestrian had been struck.

Jake paused as he recalled a moment in Algeria's Casbah when he had gazed upon a dead member of al-Qaeda who had the same type of tattoo on the palm of his left hand. It was a small jihadist flag that was affiliated to an Islamic terrorist organization.

Jake quickly looked back at the location where he had placed the driver on the sidewalk. But all he saw were bewildered looking bystanders pointing down an adjacent alleyway. The driver was no longer among the crowd, had gained consciousness, then disappeared in the darkened alley.

Janet had already left Jake's side and was cradling the head of the unfortunate individual that had been hit. The man was dazed but slowly responded to her questions.

"Are you okay? Please don't attempt to move. We have medical assistance responding," Janet said as she used her apron to wipe blood from the victim's forehead.

The man slowly opened his eyes. "I have a slight pain in my right leg, but can you please help me get up?"

Janet uttered, "No, no you must stay down and limit your movements." But her demands were ignored and the man gradually, though painfully, stood.

Jake had crossed the street and was walking toward Janet, shaking his head and reaching out to steady the victim. "Will there ever be a day that evil is not chasin' your soul?"

Janet was stunned by Jake's blunt statement. "Jake, that's so cruel to say to this poor man!"

"Sorry Miss Janet," Jake said while continuing to shake his head. "This man and I go way back in time. The near-death experiences we have shared would make your head spin."

Jake wrapped his big arm around Mitch's waist to steady him and then asked, "Other than the pain in your leg and a little blood on your face, are you okay?"

Mitch rubbed his forehead and noticed the crimson color on his hand. He took a deep breath, shook his head, knowing he had again cheated death. "I'm okay Jake, just a little shook up and bruised."

Jake helped Mitch sit on a bench that was leaning against an old cobblestone wall across the street from the tobacco shop.

"So, tell me Colonel, where the hell were you headin' in such a rush? And why didn't you notice the car as you dashed across King Street?"

Mitch slowly raised his head and looked Jake directly in his eyes. "Jake, that car came directly at me. I was just stepping off the sidewalk when the son of a bitch hit me. He definitely steered into the oncoming lane to get me. Then he must have oversteered, losing control of his car while attempting to accelerate and escape."

Jake rubbed his chin. "So that answers my questions about the crash and the tattoo."

"What do you mean, Jake? What does a tattoo have to do with this?"

Jake glanced down at Mitch and then noticed quite a few bystanders gathering nearby. "Now is not the time or place for me to answer your questions."

Janet, in the meantime, had run to the med techs and directed them to Mitch. As they began to examine him, he was not in the mood to waste any more time.

"Please stop what you're doing. I'm okay except for a few bumps and scraps. Aren't there other victims in this town that need your skills more than me?"

Jake could tell that Mitch was extremely anxious, and that there was something else burning within him that he had not revealed.

"What is it, Colonel? There's somethin' else that troubles you much more than your pain from bein' hit."

Mitch slowly pushed the med techs away and grabbed Jake's arm while rising from the bench. He leaned very close to his old friend and whispered with a desperate tone, "They've got Abella! I'm afraid Seth Hunt will kill her before I can attempt a rescue."

Jake's head snapped back as he straightened from leaning over to hear what Mitch was saying. Reality slammed into his consciousness, and Jake realized that the driver with the Islamic tattoo was a member of the GSPC and Hunt's hitman. He cringed at the thought of what evil Hunt had planned for Abella now that he had her. Torture, rape, and finally death would not be the final chapter in Abella's life if Jake had anything to do with it.

"Little lady, I have an immediate request," Jake said to Janet. "You take care of the police and their reports. The colonel's name is Mitch Ross, and if they have more questions tell them to read about him in the *Washington Post*. It's the same colonel that beat the Congressional Intelligence Committee awhile back. I promise I will visit you in a few days, God willin', to replace that Cohiba you dropped. But the colonel and I must depart immediately."

Janet quickly responded, "Wait, what?" But it was too late.

Jake had already turned and partially lifted Mitch onto his back. They headed in the direction of the Nautical House restaurant and bar adjacent to the Potomac River.

- • - •

As Mitch hobbled, with Jake's assistance, he informed his big friend that he knew where Abella was being held. Also that it was quite a coincidence that just prior to being hit he was desperately looking for Jake and a potential vehicle to drive.

"Colonel, not to worry. A friend has allowed me to use his old pickup truck. It ain't much to look at, but it has one helluva big V8 engine that'll get us to where we need to go, pronto!"

Mitch gave Jake a thumbs up and then asked, "Jake, what about the tattoo you mentioned just before the med techs began to bother me?"

Jake ignored the question and tightened his grip around Mitch's waist as they began to slowly ascend the steps to the Nautical House.

As they limped into the restaurant Jake immediately turned toward the bar while practically carrying Mitch. He slowly lowered Mitch into a booth then the big man went to order drinks.

"Two cool drafts pronto. We're burnin' daylight and we gotta get on the road ASAP!" The bartender recognized Jake and immediately began dispensing the beer in large mugs.

, "Okay Jake, before we make a game plan while consuming this beer, I'm going to ask you one more time. Why the hell is a tattoo so important to all of this?"

Jake slowly looked around the bar making sure no one could hear their conversation. "Colonel, the man that hit you had the exact Islamic tattoo in the palm of his left hand as did many of those that we fought in the Casbah. They are followers of the GSPC. I'm betting they're using Abella as bait and they have a small army of radicals waitin' for us!"

48

Seth Hunt moved closer to Abella in the small one room cabin. The duct tape had been removed from her wrist and ankles, replaced by zip ties, though she still had tape on her mouth. Hunt dismissed her kidnappers and then pulled a large knife from a desk drawer adjacent to where he was standing. Abella attempted to scream, but her parched throat could only produce a slight whimper.

Hunt slowly eyed Abella, then with a lightening quick movement sliced her blouse open revealing her soft pink bra. He smiled when he noticed Abella's embarrassment. Then his fiendish gaze settled on her breasts. With a quick downward thrust of the knife, the bra was sliced from her body, and it fell to her feet.

Abella shook violently as she followed Hunt's eyes moving down to her waist. He noticed her drawstring tied shorts and with an upward movement of the knife cut the string. Before Abella realized what had happened the shorts dropped to her zip-tied ankles.

"Well, well my lovely lady, you don't seem too dangerous with your hands and feet tied. Let me help you with your trembling lips by putting a strip of duct tape across your mouth." Hunt reached into the opened desk drawer pulling out the tape. He momentarily lay the knife down and ripped off a portion placing it across Abella's lips.

"Now that's much better, don't you think? Also, it is quite difficult for me to stand here because you are so damn alluring. Obviously, we both are aware that you are only wearing what the infidel world would call a small reddish pink thong. But although your nakedness is extremely inviting, you sicken me because of what you and that colonel have done to my jihadist plans." Hunt slowly walked with a limp examining her female treasures. He picked up his knife and placed the tip on her throat. A small droplet of blood dripped along the length of the blade. The bleeding excited Hunt and he began to hysterically laugh and yell.

"Yes, you are definitely the ultimate cheese that will lure that infidel scum of a rat Mitch Ross to this cabin. I'll delight in the moments prior to his death as he sees your nakedness on display for all to enjoy. He will be enraged while contemplating what I might have done to you sexually. What he doesn't realize is that I would never soil my being with the impure body of an infidel female. But remember this, if I find that you are not obeying my every command, then I will have no other recourse but to allow my guards to pleasure themselves with your body! Do you understand?"

— • — •

Jake and Mitch had been on the road for several hours and were passing through Indianapolis. As promised, Jake was keeping the speed of the pickup truck well above the speed limit.

Jake momentarily looked at Mitch and ask, "Colonel, do you have any idea where that cabin might be in Fontana?"

The question snapped Mitch out of his thoughts of what Hunt might be doing to Abella. He paused for a moment and then replied, "From my understanding, the town of Fontana is small, there shouldn't be many isolated cabins."

"Do you think we should contact the local Fontana authorities so they can begin the search prior to our arrival?" Jake asked.

"Absolutely not!" Mitch scolded. "My fear is that if Hunt suspects that there are others involved in the search for Abella, he will torture and kill her immediately. No, there will only be you and I to track him down. We must take him by surprise and hope Abella is still alive."

"Do you think Hunt is doing this just to get revenge?" Jake asked.

I haven't exactly pinpointed Hunt's reason for returning to the United States, but I feel it's much more than to kill me. I honestly think that he is here to wound America. Why I feel this way, I'm not sure. But before we kill him, I will make sure he confesses!"

Jake pressed hard on the gas pedal at the thought of Abella's imminent demise. They were approaching Lake Michigan and Chicago.

After they had worked their way through the myriad of highways and expressways that intersect the magnificent city by the lake, Jake wanted to stop to gather themselves before they launched into rescue mode.

"Colonel, we need to pull over and take a breather. I know a small park along a river in a village called Fox River Grove near the Wisconsin border. I had relatives who lived there years ago before they moved and joined my folks in Louisville."

As they entered the small village off Northwest Highway, Jake stopped and picked up a few burgers and drinks. Then they proceeded to the park.

Mitch, although anxious to get to Fontana, knew that they needed a break and discuss further details of the plan.

"Colonel, we've not discussed what firepower we might need. I reckon that you either have none or forgot to tuck it away in your belongings that you brought."

"Shit, you're completely correct. In my haste I forgot to pack any form of weaponry. Even the old flintlock of Major Phillips is still in my overcoat pocket hanging behind my front door."

Jake rubbed his chin while looking out at the river. "Not to worry my old friend, I brought along two .9 mm pistols, a Beretta and a Glock. Either one is more than capable to complete the job of planting a lead sedative between the eyes of Hunt!"

As the pickup truck slowly entered the outskirts of Fontana, Mitch and Jake realized that they had to be very careful who they talked to and where they stopped. They anticipated Hunt, more than likely, had his small army spread out in the area awaiting Mitch's arrival.

Also, Mitch knew that although he needed to find Abella as quickly as possible, one thoughtless mistake could lead him into an ambush and death.

As Mitch and Jake inched along the two-lane rural road leading into town, Jake spied a group of teenage boys playing touch football in a park. He quickly pulled over and told Mitch to stay in the truck and keep his head down.

"Wait Jake, what the hell are you doing?"

"Colonel, do you have any clue where there are cabins in this town? I sure as hell don't, but I'm almost positive those boys playing football do."

Jake walked toward the field picking up one of the spare balls. The teens stopped playing when they saw the big man approaching.

"Hey, you two go out for a long pass. Trust me, I'll hit one of you for a touchdown." Jake said.

They didn't question and two of the young teens sprinted toward the end of the park.

Jake faded back and threw a clothesline pass that covered at least sixty yards. The ball hit one of the teenagers directly in the chest as he was running.

The teens stood in awe as they looked up at Jake.

"Sir, where did you learn to throw a football like that?" one of the timid boys asked. Jake looked at his admiring audience. "While attending the University of Louisville in Kentucky. I played varsity football four years at that fine institution." Another teen asked, "Did you go on to the pros?"

"Nah, I went to work for Uncle Sam and that ended my football dreams. I gotta get going, fellas, but before I do can you tell me if there are any remote cabins near here? I am supposed to meet a couple of buddies to do some fishing, but I forgot to write down the exact address."

The boys shrugged warily.

"Lots of places to fish around here," one said.

"My buddies are driving a black van. Any of you see that?"

A teenage girl who had been sitting on a bench watching the boys play, overheard Jake's question and moved closer to the group.

"You asked about a black van and a cabin mister?"

"Yes!"

The young girl smiled. "There's a dirt road that runs near my house. It's a little overgrown with tree limbs and vines, but if you follow it about a mile to where it ends, there's an old cabin. No one ever travels down that road anymore, except yesterday I was looking out my bedroom window and saw a black van heading down that road. Looked like there were a couple men in there, but I couldn't say for sure."

"Young lady, is there any chance that you would be so kind as to give me directions? I'm already late meeting my friends at the cabin."

"Actually, you can see it from here," the girl said. "Look up at that large hill near the lake that is covered with trees. You can just about see the gray-blue colored house among the pine and spruce. It'll take about ten minutes to get there from here."

Before heading back to the pickup, Jake handed the girl twenty dollars. "Now why don't y'all go get some ice cream and kickback for a while."

"Jake, I was just about ready to get out of this damn truck and find out what the hell you were up to!" Mitch said upon his friend's return. "All I saw was you wasting time while throwing a damn football to kids and then giving that young girl money!"

"Now, now Colonel. I actually had a plan and believe it or not it worked. I know where the cabin is!" Jake pointed at the distant house shrouded in the trees on the hill.

"You sly dog. Good work," Mitch said.

"Thanks Colonel. But we still need a plan. What are you thinking?"

Jake reached behind the seat of the pickup and pulled out a small, zippered bag that appeared containing the two handguns Jake had brought. Mitch stuffed the Glock into his trouser pocket and took a hard long look in the direction of the house on the hill. Then he turned toward Jake with an unyielding stare.

"I want you to drop me off at the base of the hill among the densest group of trees. I'll climb the hill along the lakeside. You'll take the opposite side of the hill. Make sure you ditch the truck, but somewhere that I can locate when Abella and I are running from the cabin. God willing! I'll give you thirty minutes to find the cabin on foot. If I suspect that you were delayed or captured, I'm not waiting. I'll get into that cabin, kill Hunt, and rescue Abella."

Jake knew that there would be no arguing or questioning Mitch. Although the plan lacked detail, time was fleeting, and they had to move. He started the truck and drove to the location where Mitch had described.

Mitch turned to Jake before departing, reaching out and grasping his friend's forearm. "Jake, if for some reason this doesn't turnout as we hoped, remember you have always been in my heart and the brother that I never had."

Mitch opened the door and quickly sprinted into the trees disappearing in their darkness.

- • - •

Mitch concealed himself behind bushes and trees as he approached a large blue house. He could see the dirt road that was nearby just as the young girl had described. But what caught his attention were the fresh tire tracks leading to the cabin, and hopefully Abella. Mitch took a deep breath to calm his nerves and stayed within the darkness of the dense trees. It was one mile to the cabin.

Mitch carefully weaved from tree to tree attempting to avoid Hunt's security guards who, he figured, would be waiting for him. There was a slight breeze that blew off Lake Geneva, rustling the trees and concealing any noise that Mitch might make as he weaved through the trees. He caught the aroma of a cigarette and immediately froze behind a thick tall pine.

Damn it, I'm being too careless! The person smoking isn't far from my location. And judging by the foul unusual odor, I don't believe it's American tobacco, Mitch thought.

He squatted, listening for activity, but the wind and stirring tree leaves muffled any sounds.

I can't wait much longer and do nothing! Mitch frantically thought.

A slight gust blew a large low hanging pine branch into Mitch's face as he was crouching behind the tree. It was then that he realized what he needed to do.

Cautiously, Mitch began to climb the large branch and discovered that it was more than ample to cradle his weight. He continued up the tree until he could see the lake, the cabin, the black van, and most importantly where the cigarette smoke was coming from.

Mitch's thoughts slowly drifted back to Algeria and the Casbah. *Don't make any stupid mistakes this time, Mitch! If I lose Abella I lose my life. I can't let Hunt escape again. Thank God most Algerians smoke cheap cigarettes.*

As he carefully surveyed the area, the breeze subsided, allowing Mitch to concentrate on the exact location of the cigarette smoke.

What the hell. Two places where there's smoke! One near my area of the hill and the other closer to the cabin. Maybe Hunt's security guards prefer the view of the lake. But I suspect that there are many more than just these two bastards guarding this place.

Mitch descended from his commanding view in the tree. He waited a few moments and then moved toward the security guard.

Mitch thought of removing the gun from his trouser pocket, but reconsidered knowing if shots were fired, it would send an immediate alarm to that sociopath Hunt.

Gotta keep my head in the game, can't react purely on emotions. God willing, I hope and pray that Abella is still alive. Somehow, I've got to carefully and quietly take out these guards.

49

Hunt was casually leaning back in an old wooden chair with his feet up on a dust covered parched pinewood desk. He carefully maneuvered the tip of a large knife as he cleaned his fingernails. From time to time he would glance at Abella who was still standing and bound at the ankles and wrists.

Hunt could not stop admiring her nakedness, deliberately licking his lips so she would notice. She stood defiantly staring at him with extreme hatred and revulsion. Finally, Hunt broke the silence by sliding the knife into a small desk drawer, then folding his hands on his chest.

"Well, well my little beautiful captive. The sun will soon be fading, and your hero has not appeared. Hmmm, perhaps I overestimated his love for you. It is unfortunate for both of us. I so wanted to see his reaction when he noticed your nakedness just before I killed him. His thoughts, I'm sure, would be limitless of what I had potentially done to you as my sexual toy."

Hunt hysterically laughed, putting his hand over his mouth to muffle his outburst.

"Little does your colonel know that your nakedness nauseates me and I'm tiring of seeing the sweat drip off your breasts. In fact, you disgust me!"

Hunt lowered his feet to the floor and limped over to Abella, putting his face very close to hers. He reached up and ripped the tape from her mouth.

"So, do you have any reply to what I've just said?"

Abella gasped before responding. Hunt began to laugh again, then looked into Abella's eyes with disgust and said, "You weak imbecilic female, answer my question!"

Abella stared at him with ultimate contempt then she angrily replied, "You want me to respond to your bullshit? Okay, I'll play your game. My answer to your question is, I REALLY NEED TO PISS!" Urine gushed through her thin thong and splashed on the floor spraying onto Hunt's shoes, trousers, hands, and arms.

Hunt jumped backward and hit the desk with extreme force, losing his footing and cartwheeling over the old piece of furniture. His head violently hit the log wall of the cabin rendering him unconscious and face down on the floor.

Abella was shocked Hunt had been disabled. She feared that within moments he would regain consciousness and rise from the floor furiously out of control. She realized that what she had done to him would more than likely result in her torture, or worse. She frantically struggled to loosen her secured wrists and ankles, but with no success. As she intently gazed at Hunt's motionless body there was no sign of life. All that Abella heard was the light breeze rattling a few loose boards of the cabin.

- • - •

Hunt slowly began to moan and move as he regained consciousness. He rubbed the back of his head, attempting piece together what had happened. Once his mind cleared, he sluggishly sat up shaking his head as if to reset his bearings. Then he gradually looked up at Abella through bloodshot eyes. His mouth trembled as he spoke incoherently. Slowly pushing himself from the floor, Abella could see the impending wrath in his every movement. He was transforming into a diabolical madman.

Before Abella could move or scream out, Hunt flew at her with raised fists to crush against her face. Abella cringed while closing her eyes anticipating the impact. But there was nothing except the sound of silence. She slowly opened her eyes and was shocked at seeing Hunt's face just inches away from her. Abella smelled his vile breath as their lips almost touched. She instinctively bent backward, and without thinking she spat into his face.

Hunt's complexion turned to scarlet red, and he began to violently shake with anger. His mind was now thinking of ways to kill her. But as quickly as it occurred, the madman oddly and strangely changed. He stopped his movements and with a sinister smile calmly looked at Abella.

"So, let's see if those breasts of yours will actually lactate?"

Before Abella could comprehend his statement, Hunt swiftly raised his hands and grabbed both of her breasts. He crushed them with such force she screamed in agony. Her knees began to buckle under the extreme pain, but Abella willed herself to stand firm. She was not going to let him see her weakness.

Once Hunt released his grip, he calmly smiled approvingly. Then he replaced the tape over Abella's mouth and turned from her muted sobbing. He casually sat in the desk chair as if nothing had happened. Then removed the knife from the drawer and began to clean his fingernails.

50

Mitch slowly approached a guard who had been startled by a scream coming from the direction of the cabin.

The scream confirmed to Mitch that Abella was in the cabin, and he prayed that she was still alive. *Oh God, please help me save Abella!* Mitch thought.

The guard's head instinctively turned in the direction of the scream. He smiled broadly knowing that Hunt was obviously abusing his beautiful captive. He raised his cigarette to his lips, inhaling while waiting for another scream.

Mitch pulled the pistol from his trousers, slightly squatted, and darted from one tree to another. He was now within a few yards of the guard. Mitch paused, taking in a deep breath, then charged the guard from behind, striking him violently on the head with his handgun. The guard crumpled as his cigarette dropped from his lips and was crushed under the weight of his body. Mitch cautiously bent over and pulled the .9mm handgun from the guard's holster. He shoved it in his trouser pocket and turned toward the scent of the second cigarette.

Cautiously, he darted from bushes to trees as the aroma of smoke became stronger. But unfortunately, a second guard had heard Mitch's approach and drew his pistol. Mitch froze behind a bush and noticed the terrorist squatting and slowly aiming his gun at a thicket of overgrown wild shrubs.

The guard nervously called out in broken English, "Stand or I shoot you dead!"

Mitch silently cursed himself for being careless as the guard moved toward the shrubs. Mitch didn't want gunfire that would alert Hunt so he desperately looked for an item that would distract the guard. As he frantically scanned his immediate area, Mitch noticed a small stone the size of a golf ball near his foot. He slowly reached down, picking it up and held it in the palm of his hand.

The guard was cautiously approaching and Mitch was now close enough to notice the nervous shaking of the man. Waiting for the precise moment to strike, Mitch paused until the man was within a few feet. Then he quickly flung the stone directly at the guard's face and then lurched to the left to avoid any potential gunfire from the guard.

The stone ricocheted off the terrorist's forehead. Blood splattered into the man's eyes and down his face. He cried in pain while staggering, dropping his pistol, as he raised his hands to cradle his head.

Mitch immediately tackled the wounded man. He forcefully pressed his pistol into the guard's neck, then said in French so there would be no misunderstanding.

"If you so much as squeal I'll blow your head off!"

Mitch grabbed the terrorist's gun that lay on the ground and ordered the guard to stand.

"Remove your belt, shirt, shoes, socks, and trousers now!"

The wounded man quickly obeyed. Once disrobed, Mitch ordered the man to turn around and put his hands behind his back. Taking the shirt, Mitch tied it tightly around the terrorist's wrists. Then he demanded the guard to back into a thin pine tree. Mitch took the trousers and wrapped them around the man's ankles and secured them to the base of the tree. Finally, he grabbed the belt looping it around the tree and the guard's tied wrists. Mitch then grabbed the filthy soiled socks and stuffed them deep into the mouth of the now partially naked man. The captive began to gag as Mitch continued to push the socks deeper into his mouth.

Mitch turned toward the cabin and cautiously maneuvered toward it's partially collapsed porch. He was still circumspect that perhaps there were more guards protecting Hunt in and around the cabin. Mitch glanced at his watch and noted that thirty minutes had elapsed since Jake dropped him off on the lake side of the hill.

As he squatted behind a tall tree devising a plan to enter the cabin, Mitch was startled by voices approaching from the far side of the old structure. He listened intently as he heard a man's North African accented voice bellow out commands.

"Keep moving scum, and make no sudden moves!"

Mitch repositioned to get a better view of what was going on. He had a sinking feeling that more than likely Jake had been captured.

- • - •

Mitch slowly lay prone as he carefully peered around the base of a large spruce. He could see Jake walking sluggishly toward the cabin as Hunt's guard aimed his pistol at the big man's head, marching him onto the porch and the front door of the cabin.

"Master, I have caught one of the infidels who has come to rescue the woman. He is a large Black man, and I have personally seen him with Colonel Ross in Alexandria. Do you want him to enter?"

"No one will enter except for that bastard Ross. He is the only trophy that I desire. But before I kill the colonel, I will personally torture him and his lady. Do what you want with the Black man, but don't allow his blood nor his body to be found near this cabin!"

After Hunt's statement there was an unsettling silence that lingered from within the old structure. The guard took a few steps toward Jake, raised his pistol aiming with both hands, and ordered him to walk back into the forest away from the cabin.

As the two men continued to move into the dark dense growth of trees, the guard noticed a large, uprooted pine tree. There was a deep gaping trench like hole where once stood the tree. The guard commanded Jake to kneel near the edge of the pit and then the terrorist slowly removed an extended cylindrical item from his pocket. He turned his gun and gradually screwed the cylinder onto the end of the barrel of the pistol. Jake bowed his head and began to pray as he took a deep breath and waited for the inevitable.

Mitch had been closely watching from a distance and proceeded in the direction of where Jake was kneeling. He made sure that his position was concealed by the thick undergrowth of the forest.

Shit, that guard is screwing a silencer onto his gun. He plans to take Jake out right here in the forest! Mitch gingerly stepped toward Jake and the guard, who was standing over and just behind Jake. He intended to shoot Jake in the head and kick his lifeless body into the large hole. Slowly the terrorist raised his gun, but Mitch had already taken aim and was ready to pull the trigger. Then another loud scream came from the cabin. Mitch recognized Abella's voice! He fired as he turned and sprinted toward the dilapidated building with a pistol in each hand.

"Well now, I'm sure your hero will be appearing here in the cabin shortly. Let's give him a little more incentive so there will be no doubt he will take center stage." Hunt began to laugh as he casually stood and took a few limping steps from behind the desk. He reached into his pocket and pulled out a packet of cigarettes.

Striking a match with his fingernail, the flame flared in brilliance in the semi-darkened room. Hunt slowly inhaled as the match brought the cigarette to life and Hunt could feel the warmth of the smoke as it entered his lungs, blowing the smoke into Abella's face.

Hunt repeated the act numerous times until Abella began to choke. Then he stared deeply into her eyes with a condescending sneer. With the cigarette clenched between his teeth, he took one last draw and spit it out of his mouth. The burning tobacco drifted toward the floor and settled on Abella's bare feet that were still bound at the ankles.

Abella screamed out in agony as the cigarette burned deep into her flesh, attempting to shift her feet to remove the smoldering embers. After what seemed to be an eternity, she took desperate measures and began to spit and urinate. The fluids splashed onto her feet and eventually extinguish the burning residue.

Hunt smiled each time Abella screamed. He knew her voice would reverberate throughout the forest and draw Mitch to the cabin like a rat to cheese in a trap.

Then they heard a gunshot and Hunt looked at Abella and said, "Today is turning into one of the greatest moments of my jihad! Ross's slave has just been killed and soon your lover boy will follow him to eternal damnation. And later, America will be on her knees severely wounded!"

Mitch's bullet grazed the chin of the guard. As the wounded terrorist lost his footing while grabbing his bloodied face, Jake quickly seized the man's right ankle and pulled him into the large pit. He leaped onto the guard and began to beat him.

In the meantime, Mitch was still running toward the cabin. He had a fleeting thought that there might be other guards lurking nearby.

If anyone attempts to stop me at this point, I'll fight them to the death. I can't waste any more time. I've got to get to Abella!

As he approached the cabin, he realized that the only entrance was the front door. Mitch wanted desperately to catch Hunt unaware, but he feared that the decrepit steps would reveal his presence. To his amazement, Mitch cleared the steps without a sound and was only a few feet from the door. He slowly reached out cautiously squeezing the rusted latch when a gut-wrenching cry came from the edge of the forest.

"Master, master he is near!"

Mitch spun around and saw a man staggering, his face completely covered in blood. The man struggled to stand but failed and fell forward. There was no further movement and he appeared to have taken his last breath.

Damn him, damn him to hell! That's the guard I struck in the head with my pistol. I thought the bastard was dead! Mitch clenched his jaw, realizing that his surprise entry to the cabin had been ruined.

In desperation, he turned with guns in both hands and slammed his body against the rotting door. The wood splintered and disintegrated as Mitch crashed into the cabin. As his eyes quickly focused in the dimly lit room. He stared in disbelief at a bound, gagged, and practically naked Abella! She attempted to yell out, but it was too late.

Hunt was ready. He had moved near the desk away from the door. He was casually leaning against the log wall pointing his .45 caliber Colt pistol at Mitch's head. Hunt felt overjoyed and began to hysterically laugh, overcome by elation.

"Welcome Colonel, it's been such a long road since the Casbah. But now the three of us are all together again, and soon you and Miss Abella will be bowing at the feet of Allah!" Hunt motioned for Mitch to drop the guns and kick them over toward the desk.

Mitch didn't care about the words from Hunt, nor the pistol aimed at his head. He ripped off his shirt and draped it over the nakedness of Abella's body. Then he kissed her lightly on the cheek while whispering in her ear.

"Don't worry, we'll get out of this mess somehow."

She lurched forward wanting to feel the warmth of Mitch's body but knew any false moves could potentially enrage Hunt.

While Mitch stood defiantly staring at Hunt, the diabolical madman calmly threw four large black zip ties in his direction.

"Pick them up and attach them tightly around your ankles. If you don't follow my directions, I'll blow Abella's head completely off her body."

Hunt smiled as he slowly moved the gun from where Mitch stood to Abella's head. He remained leaning against the wall. Once Mitch's ankles had been bound Hunt directed him to kneel.

"Colonel, get on your knees and face your lady! Now put your hands together behind your back. Don't make any false moves. Remember what I just said. If you do something foolish a bullet will enter sweet Abella's forehead and splatter her brains all over the cabin walls!"

Hunt grabbed four more zip ties, putting them around Mitch's wrists sinching them until he grimaced in pain.

Mitch was only a few feet away from Abella, but under the circumstances he felt miles apart. He slowly looked up as she was still sobbing and attempting to say something, her mouth still taped. Mitch felt worthless and knew that barring any miracle, this was how it would end for he and Abella.

Hunt moved from the wall where he had been standing and sat slowly in the chair adjacent to the desk. He carefully examined his

Colt pistol, making sure there was a bullet in the chamber and the magazine was tightly secured. He raised it up with almost a graceful swing of his right arm. Looking down the barrel and focusing on the back of Mitch's head. Then Hunt lowered it and rested the gun on his right thigh.

"Colonel Ross, before I kill you, I must tell you why I left the security of Algeria. I was ordered by my master, Osama bin Laden, to rendezvous with warriors of the jihad that were living here in your shit-stained country. My task was to make sure they were in training north of Chicago. It has been so simple and without a misstep except when you would interfere with our plans. But now the training is complete, and you are no longer relevant. I have conquered you on your own soil and now I humiliate you as my final act of revenge."

The tape over Abella's mouth had loosened from the moister of Abella's tears, and she screamed, "Please no! Have mercy on us. We will go far away and cause you no further harm."

Hunt laughed then abruptly stopped.

"Shut up whore. You're not worthy to talk to me and ask for mercy. Ask Allah when you're in his presence in a few moments."

Hunt casually looked at his wristwatch and broadly smiled.

"Colonel, you have been so taken up by your quest to find your slut, that you have no clue what Osama bin Laden and I have done. This morning at approximately eight forty-five, Satan's landmark buildings in New York City were struck by our warrior heroes of the jihad. They commandeered jetliners full of infidel passengers and used them as giant guided missiles. Yes, those two jets struck and set ablaze the Twin Towers of the World Trade Center in Manhattan. In less than two hours, both buildings have collapsed in massive clouds of dust killing thousands of scum infidels. But it doesn't end at that. Our third jet destroyed the Western face of Satan's giant military headquarters . . . the Pentagon!"

"What the fuck are you talking about?" Mitch yelled.

Hunt slowly cleared his throat and calmly answered.

"Today has been victorious for our jihad against the US! I'm sure we have killed more Americans than was lost on the beaches of Normandy during D-Day! You have no clue what I'm talking about, but I have been updated by my guards hourly. They were ordered to walk along the Fontana shoreline and listen to the conversations. Or watch a local bar television broadcast of the news that is dominating all worldly communications. Every moment since the first jet struck, the entire world has been focused on our victory! All flights have stopped over America and the world is in shock. But I'm sure my jihadist brethren are joyously dancing in the streets. Today's attacks are beyond our most gratifying expectations. I have fulfilled my journey on this earth, and if I must die today, I die the happiest and most satisfied man!"

Mitch's mind was still spinning with questions, but as much as he distrusted Hunt, he realized something catastrophic was happening to America, and he had been a pawn in a great ploy. A distraction. Bait for the terrorists.

Mitch felt the gun barrel rest against the back of his head. He looked up at Abella and said, "Never forget my love for you."

Hunt had heard enough and yelled, "Shut up infidel, your time on this earth has ended.

Allaha Akbar, Allaha Akbar, Allaha Akbar!"

51

As darkness began to descend on Lake Geneva the silence of the evening was to be abruptly shattered. A distant whisper drifted through the partially opened broken door of the cabin.

Abella's eyes widened and the wet tape upon her trembling lips fell to the cabin floor. She looked down at Mitch and noticed a small red dot on the right side of his head. She screamed, "Mitch... duck!"

But before he could move, a strange noise followed her warning as a high velocity bullet flew through the small opening of what remained of the door and ripped into its target's throat. The impact of the bullet knocked him immediately to the floor as blood splattered and the sound of desperate breathing filled the air.

What followed was an eerie silence except for the wheezing and gurgling struggle of a human. Death was within moments, yet the mortally wounded victim wanted to speak out.

Mitch was still on his knees having difficulty comprehending what had just happened. He had expected to be shot in the head. He quickly looked for blood on his body, but there was none. He slowly turned and saw Hunt struggling and bleeding, his eyes wide and his lips attempting to form words. Although Mitch's wrists and ankles were still bound, he rolled over and lay near his nemesis, listening to the whispered last words of the madman.

"You have lost. Our jihad is victorious. America will never

completely recover or forget what we have done today!"

Hunt's eyes rolled up into their sockets. He blindly reached out and grabbed Mitch's arm with a bloodstained hand. Hunt took a long deep breath and then his hand fell from Mitch's arm. There was no longer a struggle for life. Seth Hunt was now with Allah.

- • •

As Mitch and Abella attempted to rationalize what had just happened, the remnants of the door slammed open. A huge man ran toward Abella. She screamed as he pulled a large knife from his trouser pocket. Then the mysterious man spoke.

"Don't be afraid little lady, it's Jake!"

Jake quickly cut the zip ties from Abella's wrists and ankles. Then pulled Mitch's shirt tightly around her body so it would not loosen. She was shaking but immediately ran to Mitch who was still on the floor beside Hunt. Abella helped Jake cut the ties from Mitch then as he rose to his feet. She collapsed in his arms sobbing and kissing him. Then the two of them turned and wrapped their arms around Jake as they all began to cry and laugh with relief.

"Jake, what the hell happened after I fired at the guard, and you were still on your knees near the pit? Did my shot hit the guard? Where did you go? Who or what sniper made that precision shot that took out Hunt? Were there police involved?"

Jake raised his hand to silence the barrage of questions and took a few steps toward the door.

"Perhaps y'all need to step out and let the good sheriff and his staff do their work here in the cabin. Besides, I must introduce you to a lovely young lady that saved us all! Without her timely inputs I reckon I would be under arrest for attempted murder, you would be dead with a bullet in the head, and Abella most likely would have been raped and then tortured to death."

Mitch and Abella looked at each other in bewilderment. Then

turning to Jake, Abella asked, "How could a young girl accomplish such a monumental feat?"

Jake opened what was left of the door and motioned for Mitch and Abella to walk onto the porch. Then the three proceeded to the tree line where a policewoman and young girl were standing.

Jake smiled at the blonde adolescent and said, "Let me introduce you to Sarah, this brave teenager defied all odds and saved our tails. But to answer all your questions you posed to me, I believe it would be much easier if y'all hear directly from Sarah."

With that said, Sarah began to slowly unravel the mystery of how she was able to stop Seth Hunt.

"I started my day by going to our school athletic field to watch the boys play flag football. Everything was as it normally is on a Tuesday teacher workday here in Fontana. It's a day that we have off to allow the teachers to catch up on paperwork. Nothing special happened until Mr. Jake pulled up in his pickup truck and began to throw the football and talk to the guys. He was a stranger and I noticed there was another man attempting to hide in the truck. It was very odd, but there was something about Mr. Jake that seemed to be genuinely sincere.

"When he asked about a black van that had recently arrived in Fontana and something about a cabin, I knew exactly what he wanted to know. Twenty-twenty hindsight, I shouldn't have been so free with the information I gave Mr. Jake. Especially the location of my home on the hill overlooking the lake. That's why I didn't go with the boys to the ice cream store with the money Mr. Jake gave us. I ran up the hill and eventually got to my house. But I remember that I smelled something odd, it was cigarette smoke! No one smokes near my house or near the old, dilapidated cabin. But the smoke smell seemed to be stronger as I slowly made my way to the cabin. I saw several men smoking while they stood among the trees. I know all the good hiding places, so no one saw me and the men weren't paying much attention to anything anyway, but I noticed that they had very large guns.

When I got to the cabin, I hid in the shadows so no one could see me. Plus, I knew where there were large cracks in the log walls. The cracks allowed me to get a good look at what was going on inside. I saw a woman tied up and practically naked."

Abella blushed at hearing the young girl's statement. She quickly wrapped her arms around Mitch pulling him close while attempting to hide her embarrassment.

The young girl continued. "I could tell that the evil man had been torturing her and saying mean things that made the woman cry. I noticed he had a very large knife, and he also carried a pistol. I decided to return to my house, but as I was tracking back I heard the woman scream, so I returned to the cabin to see if she was okay. Shortly after, I saw a man with a gun pointing at Mr. Jake. He took Mr. Jake to the cabin, but the evil man inside told them to leave. I got the impression that the evil man wanted Mr. Jake dead. I followed them into the thick forest and the man had Mr. Jake get on his knees by a large pit. Then you appeared on my left."

Sarah pointed at Mitch. "You quickly fired a shot at the man that was about to kill Mr. Jake. You missed, but that is when Mr. Jake pulled the man into the pit and began hitting him. I ran home to call my dad on the phone and tell him what I had seen. But by the time I got to the house I noticed my dad pulling up in his patrol car. My dad is the sheriff of Fontana and I quickly told him what I had seen, and we both began to run to the cabin.

"As we approached the old log building my dad radioed for backup. It was then that we noticed Mr. Jake dragging the man he had beaten up. My dad had his hand on his gun and the other taking out his handcuffs. I could tell he was going to arrest Mr. Jake, but I quickly explained who Mr. Jake was and that we should help him. Mr. Jake basically told us what was going on in the cabin and I filled in exactly what I had seen. I took my dad and Mr. Jake to the side of the cabin, and we saw what the evil man was doing to the lady and this man."

Sarah again pointed to Mitch and Abella. "My dad told me to stay put. He lined up a clear shot and fired. My dad was a marksman in the Army. He can hit a tin can from fifty yards."

Jake bent down and gave Sarah a hug and thanked her for being so brave. They all knew that Sarah's timely actions saved their lives.

The sheriff nodded to the group. "We have had one helluva day. Terrorist attacked New York and the Pentagon. Everyone is on high alert. Your partner here showed me his credentials and explained who you are. I expect you'll be wanted back in DC promptly and that your people will clean up this mess here."

Mitch nodded. "Thank you, sheriff. Your little girl is a hero."

"Before I let you all go your separate ways, I still need to make an official report. Two people are dead, and we had an abduction."

The sheriff directed his deputy to gather the three additional testimonies.

52

The sun had set, and Lake Geneva was now a black, cool void. With their testimony complete, Jake, Mitch, and Abella were free to go with the understanding that if additional information was needed, they would be available for further questioning.

The three of them again thanked Sarah and wedged themselves onto the bench seat of the old pickup truck.

"So y'all would like to stop for a bite to eat?" Jake asked as he slowly drove the truck through town.

Abella was sitting between Jake and Mitch and began to laugh. "I'm definitely hungry, but considering my lack of clothing except for Mitch's shirt, I vote we go through a drive-up window for burgers and fries."

Jake and Mitch smiled then began to laugh at Abella's comment. But it was more than her comment that lightened the atmosphere. They all knew that for the first time in quite a while they could genuinely laugh and were totally free of the threat of Seth Hunt.

Jake reached and turned on the radio. When the radio static cleared, Jake moved the dial up and down the channels. Every channel was reporting of the tragic attack on America. What they heard was beyond belief.

Terrorists had struck the Twin Towers in New York and the Pentagon, just as Hunt had said. Thousands were dead. Airports were closed and the military on high alert. They learned that a fourth plane crashed in a field in Pennsylvania. It has been conjectured that the passengers fought with the hijackers. There is speculation that the terrorists in the fourth jet had targeted the Capitol building in Washington."

The report continued as they sat in stunned horror while listening to the traumatic news. Finally, Abella couldn't restrain herself and said with a vengeful tone, "My God, Hunt wasn't lying. I hope that worthless piece of shit is burning in hell with all his warrior buddies!"

- • - •

As they drove in silence heading back to DC, contemplating all that had happened, one overriding thought among all four was that Seth Hunt, Osama Bin Laden, and the al-Qaeda terrorists had forever changed the way Americans would live their lives.

Mitch knew that he and Abella's lives would never be the same. But perhaps that would be for the better. He leaned over and turned off the radio without saying a word. Then in the darkness and silence of the pickup, Mitch said, "I wanted to keep this a secret for a more appropriate time and place, but considering how our world has changed so rapidly in twenty-four hours I might as well let you know. I had submitted my retirement paperwork before the kidnapping of Abella. I received official notification that it has been approved. After almost thirty years of active military service, it will all come to an end. This is not exactly how I had envisioned it to end, but if Abella is by my side, life will be good!"

It took a few moments for Jake and Abella to absorb what Mitch had said, considering all they had experienced that day. But once reality settled in, Abella turned and kissed Mitch passionately. Then Jake spoke, "Congrats, Colonel! That's the best news I've heard in a long, long time. I reckon now that the dust is settlin', you and Abella will be makin' plans to move on. If ya'll would open the glove compartment, I never leave home without a little pick-me-up. Let's at least put a happy endin' to this otherwise dreadful day."

Mitch reached down and opened the glove compartment, which revealed a small silver flask. He unscrewed the top and smelled the sweet aroma of quality bourbon. He turned to Abella and said, "To the wonderful lady in my life who has given me a reason to live."

With that said, Mitch passed the flask to Abella. She raised it above her head, saluting Mitch and then took a long healthy swig of the Kentucky magic. She passed it back to him and Mitch slowly put the flask to his lips and tasted the warm soothing liquid as it pleased his parched throat. He smiled and leaned toward Abella sharing the wonderful flavor as their lips met.

Jake laughed and whispered, "I won't be partaken of that fine elixir while drivin', but please do save me a swallow for when we reach Alexandria."

Mitch and Abella smiled as the top of the flask was slowly replaced and returned to the glove compartment. Abella rested her head on Mitch's shoulder and within a few moments was sound asleep.

53

Jake stood silently watching Mitch slowly pack the saddlebags of an old Harley-Davidson. He noticed Mitch was taking an extremely long period packing and repacking items as if he didn't want to say goodbye to his old friend. Finally, Jake reached up and pulled the well-worn cigar from his mouth.

"Colonel, I truly hate to see you and Abella leave, but I know you must. But you've gotta tell me where your headin' so if I need to reach you I can."

Abella walked out of the flat across from the old Anglican Church and closed the door for the last time. She looked at Jake with tears streaming down her face. Then grabbing his arm to steady herself, she tiptoed while pulling Jake close and kissed him warmly on the cheek.

Jake felt her soft lips and the moistness of her tears as his massive arm wrapped around her waist and he gently gave her a loving hug. Releasing Abella, Jake stared at Mitch and asked again.

"Colonel, I know you don't want people to know where you two are going, but we've been through so much together and—"

Before Jake could finish, Mitch replied while helping Abella climb onto the motorcycle.

"Jake, these last few years have been some of the greatest and worst times of my life. Abella and I want to get away from all this madness. So, I reached out to some old friends, Jen and Taylor.

They've invited us to stay with them in what they call the Valley of the Mountains, for as long as we desire."

Once Abella was securely seated behind Mitch, he throttled the bike and kickstarted the engine. It roared to life as Mitch adjusted the choke and reconfirmed the position of the fuel valve. Mitch glanced up at Jake while grabbing the big man's hand and said, "We're heading on the back roads to a town nestled between mountains called Three Forks. It's far away from here and it has only one main road. Jake, if you need to find us just walk in the path of Lewis and Clark and head toward the land that the Shoshone called the Big Sky."

With that, Mitch and Abella departed and soon were out of sight except for the roar of the Harley engine in the distance.

Jake could already feel the loss of his two friends and slowly reached up and placed the last bit of his cigar to his lips and whispered while gazing at the empty road.

"Godspeed Colonel. Lord knows you deserve all the peace and quiet that you're seeking.

Godspeed!"

www.ingramcontent.com/pod-product-compliance
Lightning Source LLC
LaVergne TN
LVHW041700070526
838199LV00045B/1140